I0687802

ROCKY FOUNDATION FOR PEACE

The Life of Octavianus

Dr. Fiona Erica Nichols

First published in Australia by HiveMind Press 2021.

ISBN: 978-0-6450588-2-6

Typeset/Cover Design by – HiveMind Press.
Artwork – Brian Craddock

HiveMind Press

CONTENTS

CHAPTER ONE

The roads ran out like main arteries from the heart of Rome, stretching over thirty thousand miles to the foreign extremities of a dying Republic. The heartbeat of Rome soon ceased in a cardiac arrest of senatorial stabbings. A fog heavily laden with guilt hung in the air, the conspirators staying at the scene of the crime, as Iulius Caesar bled profusely on the stone floors of the senatorial house. As Caesar's life flashed before him, he cried with his dying breath, 'This is violence! Not you too, Brutus! Not you!' Caesar then inhaled his last breath and abruptly died.

Marcus Antonius, Caesar's leading general, took the initiative, and obtained possession of Caesar's money and state papers. This was only made possible through Calpurnia, Caesar's widow, who most likely entered the The Temple of the Vesta, a place generally forbidden to men. This templed housed the perpetual flame of Rome, and if it were extinguished by any means this meant impending doom for the city. Inside the arched temple, numerous virgins and eunuchs surrounded the perpetual flame, which was burning brightly as ever. The Vestal Virgins were protectors of the flame, and the eunuchs who accompanied them, were the protectors of their virginity. If their chastity was compromised, the penalty was death by being buried alive.

After thirty years of servitude, these élite virgins were able to retire and own land, a privilege granted to no other woman in Rome. As the flame remained protected and burnt brightly, there was still hope for all Roman people, including the women.

Marcus Aemilius Lepidus, a member of Caesar's triumvirate, held a legion of troops at the gates of Rome to prevent any further violence. Antonius, taking control of events, scheduled a meeting for the senate the next day. On the fifteenth of March 44 BCE, the sun set for one last day in the Roman Republic, for the next was the dawning of a new era.

Chaos prevailed in the senatorial house, and accusations of murder were flung about in daily conversation. Antonius stepped forward into the ensuing anarchy to calm those who were bereaved, and others who were panic stricken. There, on the marble slab before Antonius, lay Caesar's will, sealed up with its secrets. Antonius' clammy hands gently broke the seal and sweat rolled down his tanned brow. The unfurled document bequeathed a sum of money to every Roman citizen, and the public use of his gardens beyond the Tiber. This news, of-course, would please the common people of Rome, yet blood boiled in the senatorial house, jaws jutted out in displeasure, and stern gazes of judgement surrounded the last words of Caesar. Antonius' hands shook, as the words that followed revealed Caesar's chief heir to be a young, sickly country boy, named Gaius Octavius. Decimus Brutus, beloved friend to Caesar, and one of his assassins, hung his head in shame when the will revealed that he too had inherited some of the Caesarean fortune. The fortune of Rome, itself, was not too great, and the perpetual flame dimmed for a moment in the Vesta heralding impending doom. Antonius proposed a public funeral for Caesar, and volunteered himself for the public reading of the will. A tumult amongst the senators resounded, and Cassius, another assassin of Caesar, attempted to veto Antonius' proposition, in fear of another civil war between plebeians and patricians.

Brutus, although humiliated, rose to challenge the motion of Cassius, which showed favour to Antonius in the Senate House. Cicero, who was impressed by this excellent strategy, joined with Cassius and Brutus on the outskirts of the senate and placed his hands on the conspirators, calling for an amnesty for those who had killed Caesar. Antonius approved the amnesty, as did the house of senators, and he proposed to abolish the dictatorship from politics, which gained the support of all.

Adulation for Caesar increased when Roman plebeians became aware of their inheritance at the funeral. The men cheered at the kind offering an women sobbed, mourning the loss of Caesar. Antonius swallowed his pride, announcing, Octavius, the grand nephew and adopted son of Caesar, as the chief heir to hisestate. The common people flocked to pay their respects to Caesar, and exultation soon turned to cries of vengeance when they beheld the multiple stab wounds and bloodstained clothing of Caesar. The crowd's fury increased and bloody tears ran down the face of the statue of the Venus Gentrix, as she mourned her great grandson, and the loss of love in the world. The crowd was whippedinto a frenzy, and they called for justice for Caesar's murder. Antonius's confidence increased, and he smirked in pleasure, as Cassius and Brutus fled the public procession for more remote posts outside Rome. The great general puffed out his chest, straightening his posture, and the statue of Mars mirrored him. The bloody tears of Venus flowed steadily, for it was March, a monthdedicated to the elaborate honouring of Mars. Although Antonius held complete control of Rome, Cicero believed that his intention to abolish dictatorship was genuine, and the majority of senators believed that the old republic would be restored. However, as Antonius' thirst for power and wealthincreased, so too did their doubts. The crowds were quelled, and for a time there was relative quiet in Rome.

The hooves of Octavius' majestic war-horse struck the cobble stones of the wide curved streets which led into Rome from Macedonia and, with eachapproaching step, news of Octavius' return began to break the restful silence. Octavius had no idea of the inheritance left to him, and that this journey would signify his loss of innocence. The days of the journey were warm, and Octavius did not respond well to the elements, for it aggravated his health. Although, signify his loss of innocence. The days of the journey were warm, and Octavius did not respond well to the elements, for it aggravated his health. Although, Octavius was not always well, he did his best to conceal it in his manly pride, fo to show weakness was a big disadvantage. As he coughed along the way, he remembered that it was the same kind of sickness that had prevented him going to Spain with Caesar in 46 BCE. Determined to meet with Caesar, Octavius had followed the roads captured by the enemy, taking with him a small band of men, even though his health was on the mend, though still fragile. Caesar was impressed by Octavius' initiative and determination, thus making provisions for him in the will soon after.

Octavius, worn from the journey, awoke slumped over on his steed, which was plodding along at a steady pace. He adjusted himself quickly when he sawthe spectacular columns of Rome, which were merely matchsticks on the horizon at this stage. The closer he approached, the more the city loomed larger, and the intricate detail of archways and columns decorated with carved grapevines, became more apparent. Octavius entered the gates of Rome with Marcus Agrippa, his trusted school friend, who had accompanied him on the long journey from Macedonia. Inside the gates, Caesar's veterans and friends welcomed Octavius with exultation and the highest reverence. As they progressed toward the forum, which was the political, commercial, and religious centre of Rome, the common people cheered in support of his new status. Slightly confused by the clamour, Octavius progressed forward on his steed, passing a domus, a single storied building with terraces, loggias, hanging gardens and alcoves. A few minutes later, both Octavius and Agrippa stopped at the thermae, or public bath, so that they could clean themselves up before meeting with the officials and senators.

The outcome of the meeting with the senators and the officials was not as Octavius had expected. Octavius addressed Cicero with the highest respect and offered his condolences. Cicero, although distrusting of Octavius, took his hand, and smilingly addressed him, saying: 'It is indeed a pleasure to meet with the young heir to Casar's estate.'
Octavius thanked him, in order to be polite, but could tell that his tone was not at all genuine. Although Octavius felt shocked that he had inherited Caesar's fortune, but in his manly pride he concealed his disbelief. When Caesar's adopted son caught sight of Antonius on the steps, with arms folded, and the statue of Mars looming behind him, he felt uneasy. It was suspected that Antonius was stricken with grief over Caesar's death, but his true intentions were to take control of the republic. Octavius outstretched his arms approaching Antonius, but his posture did not change. Octavius, somewhat disconcerted by the experience, looked at Agrippa, then at Antonius, and acted In a more formal manner, offering his condolences. Agrippa was a loyal friend, and was very suspicious of Antonius, so therefore did not let him out of his sight.

Had you been there, your experience may havebeen very different. You could have been looking down into one of the cobble stone streets from the terrace of a domus. You might have even seen Octavius plodding along on his horse and been part of the excitement cheering him on. Or perhaps you had served in the Gallic wars or in Spain under the supreme command of Caesar, and naturally showed your allegiance to Octavius. Or maybe you might have been one of the senators meeting Octavius at the Forum, realising you were having doubts about his youthful intentions. If you had been looking out of the Venus Genetrix, you would wonder why there was so much hatred in the world and had you been Octavius, you would have found a surprise at every turn. You might have felt uneasy about some people's response to you at the Forum, and asked yourself what was going on. And if you had been visiting Rome that day, you would realise that something was amiss, and that Antonius' actions were not quite right.

Antonius, opposed to the return of Octavius, was smug in the knowledge that he done his best to maintain control in Rome, but talk among the senators echoed that his thirst for wealth and power was too much like that of a dictator. However, Octavius was shrewd and thought carefully about every move he made because of the watchful eyes in Rome. After learning that Caesar had adopted him, Octavius attempted to have his adoption made legally valid, which Antonius blocked because he did not wish to hand over the deceased Caesar's dwi dling funds. Obliged to honour his father's legacy, Octavius was forced to borrow money so that he was able to pay every Roman citizen the inheritance left to them. In a private room of the forum with Agrippa, Octavius held his head, pacing back and forth with worry.

'Dear Marcus, my trusted friend, I am sick with worry and unable to pay this debt left to me because of Antonius. What ever will I do?'

Agrippa responded to reassure him: 'Sweet Octavius, you already have more land than you need. Sell your spare property, so that those less fortunate than you might get their sevety-five denarii'

'*Marcus,*' Octavius said, pausing, 'It is not simply enough meet the needs of Uncle Iulius. I have to do something great to honour him yet surpass him. Something that proves me to be the ultimate heir to Caesar and not just a sickly coun-

try boy, but I have to be careful, as my parents warned me. The thrust of a knife cannot be allowed to penetrate my body. I must outlive and outsmart people's expectations'. Agrippa had a sudden idea, 'The Venus Genetrix', he said, and paused. 'The Venus Genetrix is your answer. Have a festival to honour her in the name of the deified Caesar, and all will be in your favour.'
Octavius nodded his head approvingly and smiled.
'Yes, of course. Now it is just a matter of funding.'

Upon paying the populace their inheritance, Octavius won the favour of the masses. The idea of the festival in honour of the Venus Genetrix excited all people, and crowds applauded the approaching event. On the first day of the festivity, Livy, a literary scholar, looked to the heavens, and pulling out his stylus, inscribed the following words into his wax tablet:

Ludis Veneris Genetricis, quos pro collegio fecit, stella horas undecima crinita sub septentrionis sidere exorta convertit omnium oculos. Quod sidus quia ludis Veneris apparuit, divo Iulio insigne capitis consecrari placuit. (Livy, 1959, p.57).

These words would later be immortalised, and translated into many tongues, including English, so that the whole world would remember the message, which read:

At the festival of Mother Venus, which he conducted for the college, a comet appearing at the eleventh hour under the constellation of the Bear drew the eyes of everyone. Since this star appeared at the festival of Venus, it was decided to dedicate it as a crown jewel to the deified Caesar. (Livy, 1959, p.57)

The crimson tears of Venus dried up, for love was restored, and the once lovelorn heart of Rome, which housed the perpetual flame, was brighter than it had been in over two hundred years. Antonius, unimpressed by the festivities, emulated the statue of Mars, whose posture was rigid and unforgiving. In Antonius' mind Octavius was hardly a political rival, but he was increasingly irritated by the extent of Caesar's favouritism toward the young boy. Venus smiled, knowing every intention in Antonius' mind, and the sword Mars began to crumble a piece at a time, and the whole statue began to erode.

.

Antonius, sure of his victory, stood firm, believing secretly that he would be able to transform himself into Caesar even though his power was crumbling.He was blinded by his greed and could not see that the people's love of Octavius was the best weapon against his self-conceit. Whilst Antonius had control of Caesar's fortune, he did not have control of the people's love for Caesar and his son. Though Antonius seemed self-assured in public, his confidence behind closed doors was increased by resorting to the bottle, and as a man who did not know love, he bought it from a series of one night stands. Antonius' everincreasing self-indulgence was slowly chipping away at the Caesarean funds, and the wind of Rome whispered rumours of foul doings into people's ears. Suspicions amongst senators and republicans were mounting, and favour was steadily increasing for Octavius. Every time Antonius turned the corner of a cobble stone street, a series of mutterings amongst the common people followed. However, when Octavius walked amongst the people, cheers resounded, and young girls attempted to grasp on to him in adulation. As time went on, tension in the senate house increased, as republicans became aware that Antonius had no intention of ridding Rome of dictatorship, and indeed secretly longed for the day that he would be emperor.

Octavius requested that Antonius hand over all of Caesar's funds, but he refused to do so, and the statue of Mars shook his rocky head in disapproval. Mars had become tired of being called upon for useless wars, and thus decided to turn his back on Antonius, which meant that he would be forever doomed to failure. Antonius, the great general, was sure that

Mars favoured him, for he had always been victorious. Perhaps it was his intoxication that clouded his judgement, but Antonius believed that the key to all power in Rome was in the armies that lay in the Gallic provinces, which is why he had Decimus Brutus transferred to Macedonia, and took command himself of Cisalpine Gaul. Later, he also secured Transalpine Gaul for himself and managed to extend his term for five years. Additionally, Antonius arranged to transfer four Macedonian legions to his own command. Though Antonius knew he might have to wage war with Decimus Brutus to gain complete control of the area, he had set up a situation very much to his own liking, in the few months after Caesar's death. However, he forgot one small detail; that money and legions alone were not enough to achieve ultimate power. True power lay in the people, and Octavius, knowing this, secured himself that which Antonius could not- the heart of Rome. Cicero, now very distrusting of Antonius' actions, was preparing to join liberators in the East, but the situation had been made more complicated by Octavius' return to Rome. Antonius, thinking himself better, saw no threat in the young Octavius, but, Cicero, being a very insightful man, watched the situation carefully.

Octavius, disliked Antonius' outright refusal of his inheritance, so he used his oratory skills and newly assumed name Gaius Iulius Caesar Octavianus (Octavian) to win over Caesar's veterans, thus managing to recruit a private army with funds from the wealthy Equities with whom he had connections. Antonius, now aware of his decreasing power, marched north to intercept Decimus Brutus in Cisalpine Gaul, and besieged him in Mutina. However, the senate despatched consuls Hirtius and Panas in 43 BCE to thwart Antonius' attempt to take over the township. Although Octavius' recruitment of a private army was technically illegal, Cicero praised him, urging the senate to accord him with the title of Propraetorian Imperium so that he might help the consuls overcome Antonius. Such a title as Propraetorian Imperium was not usually bestowed on one as young as Octavius, for it gave him judicial power, supreme authority, and the right to flog or execute Cicero prompted the bestowal of Propraetorian Imperium in the interest of the Republic, but Decimus Brutus strongly opposed Cicero's decision although it might have saved his own life. Perhaps Brutus thought that such a manoeuvre was dangerous, as no one could challenge Octavianus' authority if Antonius died.

In Cisalpine Gaul, blood dripped from Octavianus' sword and breastplateas he stood over the dead bodies of consuls Hirtius and Panas. Octavianus cried into the heavens, and with each exasperated breath the clouds' silver linings turned to blood red in the late afternoon. Falling to his knees in the dust, his body felt as heavy as stone, and the statue of Mars began to show the wear and tear of war back in Rome. The bloody victory of Octavianus caused Antonius to retreat across the Alps like a wounded wolf who had narrowly missed the snare of a hunter. Antonius was still in one piece, but his pride was wounded. He looked to the blood stained clouds in the heavens, a cursed sign from Mars himself. Within the Senatorial House of Rome, harsh words were uttered toward Antonius as a result of Cicero's Phillipics, modelled on earlier diatribes of Demosthenes, a Greek orator, who sought to advance his political career byattacking Phillip of Macedonia.

Upon Octavianus' return to Rome, Cicero wrote a letter to the senate stating that he be praised and honoured, but the message fell on deaf ears. Octavianus, irritated by the lack of response, demanded a triumph for his victory, consulship, and payment for his soldiers, but was refused by the senate as he was technically too young for the title he now possessed. A coup d'état was acknowledged when Octavianus marched on Rome with Caesarian veterans who had a common dislike of liberators and senators; they were still loyal to the dead Caesar and his lineage. Marching on Rome was a new vogue that had been previously implemented by Marius, the great, great, uncle of Octavianus. The legions brought from Africa to protect the senate were intimidated by the sheer mass of the Caesarian legions, and soon gave passage to the senatorial house by declaring allegiance to the very enemy they were supposed to fight. On arrival, Octavianus revoked the decrees on Antonius, for it was far safer to keep his enemies close. The troops under the generals Lepidus and Antonius socialised at night, drinking wine until the early hours of the morning. Realising this, both Antonius and Lepidus joined together for a common cause, and were soon supported by the army of Plancus, a Caesarian leader present in the Gallic region. Like Rome, Cisalpine Gaul was overrun by legions, loyal to a select few, and the enemy army of Brutus was soon assimilated into the quelling chaos. Octavianus, and his eleven legions, soon joined forces with the other Caesarian legions in Bononia, which gave birth to the second triumvirate involving Antonius, Lepidus and himself. The first triumvirate had been a gentleman's agreement between Caesar and two others, but the second triumvirate of his successor, Octavianus, was far greater. Mars, tired of childish games, left the bickering schoolboys to their own devices, and groaned in frustration as the perpetual flame of Rome dimmed once more.

Octavianus stood before the mass of people in Rome with his hands linked to Antonius and Lepidus in the Forum. The crowd cheered them on and, after the other triumvirs had left, they all exclaimed; 'Gaius Iulius Caesar Octavianus' repeatedly, as his adoption as Caesar's son had been confirmed. Octavianus quietened the raucous crowds before him, and revoked the amnesty on those who had killed Caesar. The unsettled mob screamed out, 'Death to the Conspirators', and Octavianus quietened them once more, like a mother nursing her hungry babes. He announced his annulment of Cicero's Phillipics by publicly revoking the decree passed on Antonius. Cheers of exultation resounded, out of the crowd's love for Caesar and his heir. Praises of Octavianus' compassion were seen in the visual displays of drama, in the cobble stone streets, as every actor who impersonated him wanted to be him, even though the true nature of the man behind the mask had not yet been revealed.

As a result of the triumvirate, Octavianus ascended to the consulship at the tender age of twenty years, and after the triumvirate's institution, laws were enacted to confirm its term for five years. Senators were appointed by the triumvirs, and were made to vow allegiance to them, in much the same way as their soldiers did. Their proconsular commands were confirmed and Caesar was himself deified. Octavianus stood before the people of Rome in the Forum to announce Caesar's deification. The crowd went wild with the joyous news, and a passing comet honoured the Venus Genetrix, which was an official sign amongst the common people that Caesar was now in the heavens. Caesar, proud of his son, looked down on him with a gentle smile and the statue of the Venus Genetrix invited worship to those who were loyal. The love of Venus was starting to prevail, even though it was hidden in the lies and deceit of politics and ambition. The perpetual flame of Rome burnt brighter, for there was again hope. Janus, one of the principal Roman Gods and gatekeeper of the heavens, looked into the sunset of what had befallen Rome. Janus not only had the ability to look into the sunset of what had come before, but he also had the ability to look into the sunrise, the dawning of a new day, to see what would come to pass as if by some strange precognition. Janus' unique ability was made possible by his two heads, and of all the other Gods, Jupiter believed him to be the most like man in his two faced nature. Octavianus, would later close the gates of Janus, on the eastern and western sides of his shrine in the Forum, which would signify the end of war in Rome. Octavianus would later become known as Augustus, emperor of Rome and be the deified Son of God, something unheard of at this time in Rome. As if by some twisted irony he would live to witness the birth of Jesus of Nazareth, another Son of God, in the twenty-third year of his rule. However, none of this would be possible without a further struggle for power. Janus, knowing this, looked both over the chapter that had just been, and at the same time gazed into the next chapter of Octavianus' life on the horizon.

13

CHAPTER TWO

Roman blood had been shed midst victorious cries. A flurry of senatorial stabbings had taken the life of Iulius Caesar just the year before, and the Roman pulse had grown weaker. Antonius, sure of himself, believed he was bound for greatness; to be Caesar's heir, but, it was revealed that the young Octavianus would be the one to fit the part. Janus, the double headed god and gatekeeper of the heavens, viewed Rome's bloody past with one head, whilst the other foresaw the blood stained future. Mars, the god of warfare, looked upon Lepidus, Antonius and Octavianus holding hands in the Roman Forum, and shook his heavy head in disapproval. He knew that the agreement between the three generals, known as the second triumvirate, was a momentary facade for the people. The growing hatred for Octavianus flowed deep within Antonius' veins, for he was not satisfied with partial power.

It wasn't long before happy smiles in the forum of Rome turned to expressions of concern, when the three men announced that the triumvirate had been sealed by legislation. The second triumvirate was unlike Caesar's gentlemen's agreement, which was more verbal than legal, and this one would be fortified in the bloody proscriptions of 43 BCE. Octavianus' stomach turned as Antonius pressed him to commit to the pro-scriptions, and within his heart of hearts he did not want to do this. Antonius, still sure of the security of his position, thought Octavianus was an easily manipulated youth who posed little threat, and thus pressed him again. Octavianus was unyielding and with a rigid posture and crossed arms, he gave Antonius no answer. Marcus Agrippa, Octavianus' good friend and confi-dant, glared at Antonius with distrusting eyes, which narrowed the longer he stared. Antonius was disturbed by Agrippa, and puffed out his chest in a dominant manner handing Octavianus the blood list for his perusal. The list contained the names of hundreds of Senators, and those loyal to the Roman republic. Agrippa, who was not too fond of Antonius, showed him the door.

Upon viewing the documents that Antonius had giv-en him, Otavianus stood up and started to pace nervously. 'I can't do this, Marcus, yet I understand that it is necessary in order to prevent the backlash of Republicans who would have me killed like my adopted father Iulius.' Even though Agrippa disliked Antonius, he understood th list's necessity, and placed his hand on Octavianus' shoulder. 'You must, Octavianus, it is vital to ensure your survival.' 'How can I? Did you see whose name was under the letter 'C'? 'C' for Cicero. How can I commit him to death when he has done nothing but help me, publicly and privately? He helped me get here. This is Antonius' blood feud, not mine. He dislikes Cicero because of the public diatribes written about his debauched nature, which we know to be the truth.' Agrippa then advised: 'Have you forgotten, Octavianus? Cicero is a republican, and like all men, he is after what gives him the most power. He is a Patrician and under the republican system he and other men like him wield the power. Cicero could easily become a threat to you in the future, just as Antonius was in the past. Whilst you may put a man to death for being a repub-lican, you must not say what your motive is overtly. It is dan-gerous in these times to claim to be anything, but a republican.'

Octavianus frowned and thumped his forehead with his palm: 'Yes, I have thought about all that,and I have no choice, even though I do not like it.' Agrippa put his hand on Octavianus' shoulder once again, to show his sympathy.

The perpetual flame dimmed for a moment in the Vesta, and changed colour from blue to a bright red. The virgins who protected it questioned the significance of the omen, but no one could work it out. Tears of blood trickled down the stone faces of godly statues in the lava red sunset of Jupiter, and the silhouette of Mars in the Forum was foreboding. The gates of Janus were wide open on both the Eastern and Western fronts of Rome to allow legions to leave promptly in times of war.

The conceited Antonius unraveled the parchment on which the proscriptions were written, proceeding to read them publicly at the Forum. Octavianus, the better orator of the two, interjected, explaining that not all on the list were subject to death, but rather most faced confiscation of their property. On the list hundreds of senators were proscribed, along with a couple of thousand equites, the class that held most of the funds in Rome. Cicero, previous supporter of Octavianus, was sentenced to death, and even some family members of the triumvirs were proscribed as well. It was on that day, that the Roman scholar Livy inscribed the following words on his wax tablet:

> C. Caesar pacem cum Antonio et Lepido fecit ita, ut treviri rei publicae constituendae per quinquennium essent ipse et Lepidus et Antonius, et ut suos quisque inimicos proscriberent. In qua proscriptione plurimi equites Romani, CXXX senatorum nomina fuerunt, et inter eso L. Pauli, fratris M. Lepidi, et L. Caesaris, Antonii avunculi, et M. Ciceronis. (Livy, 1959, p. 152).

A statement which reads in modern English as:
Gaius Caesar made terms with [Antonius] and Lepidus,

providing that he, Lepidus, and [Antonius], should be a board of three for regulating the commonwealth for a term of five years, and that each should proscribe his personal enemies. In this proscription, there were included a very large number of Roman knights, and the names of one hundred and thirty senators, among them Lucius Paulus, the brother of Lepidus, Lucius Caesar, the uncle of [Antonius], and Marcus Cicero.(Livy, 1959, p.153).

Had you been there you there that day, you might have felt uneasy about the proscriptions. You could have been in the cobble stone streets of the Forum hearing your name being read out. Or possibly you were one of the numerous senators on the death list whose heart skipped a beat out of fear. You might have originally supported Octavianus and cheered him on in his previous victories. Or perhaps you were a middle class equite who had worked hard for your money, realising that all your worldly possessions were now about to be confiscated. Or maybe you might have been one of the distant family members of a triumvir who was accused of being an enemy of the state. Had you been that family member, you may have once been loyal to that triumvir, and felt an overwhelming sense of betrayal. Or you might have been a scholar writing down your interpretation of events carefully so that you did not appear on the proscriptions yourself. If you had been Mars, you would have felt anger toward the men who venerated you for their ill begotten success. Had you been Janus, you would have seen little hope for humankind in the near future. And had you been Venus, you would not have fathomed how your grandson Octavianus loved to hate, when you could only ever love. Or it is possible you could have been Octavianus, so full of pride that you were clouded by the illusion of being better than Antonius. Had you just been a bystander that day, you would have realised just how convoluted Roman politics really were.

In the lush green countryside, near the city of Thusculum,

two men hastily rode their mounts at full gallop. The thudding of the horses hooves made the ground tremble like a minor earthquake, and the steeds' sweat glistened in the sunlight, as they raced on to the estate of Cicero. Marcus Cicero, sleeping in the dining area, awoke to hear the sound of pounding at his door. 'Cicero! Cicero, make haste to the door, we have brought you bad tidings.' Half-dazed and confused, he rose to let the two men in. He invited them to his dining area and had his servants make the men a hot drink. The older of the two was too puffed to speak, so his younger brother, Gaius, spoke for him. 'Cicero, I bear bad tidings; the young Octavianus, Antonius and Lepidus have entered into a legal triumvirate together, and as Sulla did, they have proscribed half of Rome. Some are merely subject to banishment, or confiscation of their property. You, unfortunately, are sentenced to death for your efforts to restore the republic, though Antonius believes it is the result of you having spoiled his reputation through the Phillipics.' Cicero, longing for death, responded to Gaius by saying: 'It is not my enemies, but my jealous rivals, that have ruined me.' (Hooper, & Schwartz,1991, p. 26). Cicero thumped his heavy head into his hands, and politely asked the messengers to take their leave.

Once alone, Cicero recalled how he had longed for death many times, but not at the hand of betrayal. He searched deep within himself to find the answer to Octavianus' intentions. He found it hard to believe that Octavianus, of all people, would allow a death sentence to be passed on him. In his disbelief, he searched his mind for some clue that may have been left behind. A memory. Something. There had to be a reason. Antonius had motivation to do so, but not Octavianus, and Cicero's mind harked back to a time when he wrote a letter to Cornificius confessing as much. It read:

I returned to Rome with all the expedition that sails and oars could speed me, and the very next day after my arrival, I showed the world that I was the only man, amidst a race of abject slaves, that dared assert his freedom and independency. I inveighedindeed against the measure of [Antonius] with so much spirit and indignation, that he lost all manner of patience; and pointing the whole rage of his bacchanalian fury at my devoted head, he at first endeavoured to gain a pretence of assassinating me in the senate, but that project not succeeding, his next resource was to lay wait for my life in private. But I extricated myself from his insidious snares, and drove him all reeking with fumes of his nauseous intemperance, into the toils of Octavius. That excellent youth drew together a body of troops, in the first place, for his own and my particular defence; and in the next for that of the republic in general: which if he had not happily raised, [Antonius], in his return from Brundisium, would have spread desolation, like a wasting pestilence, around the land. ...Farewell. (Cicero,1920, p. 332-333).

The statement: '...he at first endeavoured to gain a pretence of assassinating me in the senate', echoed loudly in Cicero's head, and warning bells were resounding. He knew Antonius' motivation was serious, and that Octavianus, who previously protected him, had now turned on him like a rabid dog.

Darkness consumed Cicero's mind as Octavianus' betrayal sunk in. Tears streamed down his face, and he continued to weep through bloodshot eyes. 'Venus, you have abandoned me', he thought to himself, but nothing could have been farther from the truth, for she shook her head in disdain at Octavianus' actions. Cicero remembered how intentions had once led him to suicidal thoughts. Cicero thought of his friend, Thurii, who would often give him a listening ear in times of need, and when they were too far from each other to talk, they would exchange correspondence. At a seaport, nea Brundisium, Cicero once wrote the following letter to his confidant:

'Beloved Thurii,
As to your urging me to remain alive, you carry one point -that

I should not lay violent hand upon myself: the other you cannot bring to pass – that I should not regret my policy and my continuance in life. For what is there to attach me to it, especially if hope which accompanied me on my departure is non-existent? I will not attempt to enumerate all the miseries into which I have fallen through the extreme injustice and unprincipled conduct, not so much of my enemies, as of those who were jealous of me, because I do not wish to stir up a fresh burst of grief in myself, or invite you to share the same sorrow. I say this deliberately – that no one was ever afflicted with so heavy a calamity, that no one had ever greater cause to wish for death; while I have let slip the time when I might have sought it more creditably. Henceforth, death can never heal, it can only end my sorrow. (Hooper & Schwartz, 1991, p. 26).

Quintus Cicero, his brother, entered the kitchen where Marcus was seated, noticing his head cupped into his hands.' Brother, what sadness has taken you?' Quintus inquired. 'I don't like to see you like this.' 'I have been afflicted with a heavy calamity. Antonius, Octavianus and Lepidus have entered a legal triumvirate. I am among the many men proscribed with a death sentence. I have often longed for death, but not by the hand of my enemy.' Tears started to roll down his cheeks. Quintus, in a state of shock, questioned how this could be so, for he knew that the young Octavianus would be reluctant to do such a thing. Marcus answered: 'I have been searching the depths of my mind to work out Octavianus' reasoning, and I have found nothing. He is a deceitful lupine who has taken my heart. How could he partner up with his enemy? For this I have no understanding. I might as well take my life with my own hand. That way I can rest assured how I die, or perhaps because I long for death, I should wait here willingly for my murderers.' 'Marcus, Have you no courage? Suicide is pointless, and it is even more pointless that you should willingly accept their death sentence.' Quintus remarked. 'The republic is worth fighting for, and if one must die, it is better for a cause than for pointlessness. I hear that Brutus is gathering supporters down in Macedon. I think it best to make for Astyra, and from there to Macedon, where we can meet with the resistance. If we do not make it, we should die trying. That way our lives would have not been taken in vain. Not all hope is lost brother, never give up.' Marcus nodded his head, and the two of them packed a limited number of effects and took their leave, making way for Astyra.

On the journey that followed, Quintus became aware that they had left with such haste that he had not brought enough provisions of his own. At the next resting point the two brothers conversed and it was decided that Quintus would return home for more provisions whilst Marcus went on without him. Cicero's heart sunk as he saw his brother make way for home and tears welled in his eyes. It was a distinct possibility that Marcus might not again see his brother Quintus, and sorrowful thoughts plagued his mind, upon his brother's departure. Quintus, unlike Marcus, kept a brave face, but within his heart, he too was racked with worry. Two nights later the moon shone on the blood-stained earth, as his own slaves turned on Quintus and his son.

Upon reaching Astyra, Cicero smelt the salt in the air, and realised that he must find himself a ship to make way for his house in Capitie. The sun bore down on Cicero, punishing him with impartiality, yet the sea breezes continued to cool the crew and show favour to their vessel, thus shortening the journey. At the seaside port of Capitie where Cicero's vessel was anchored, dozens of crows were seen on the horizon coming from the temple of Apollo. Apollo, god of healing and light, did not bestow Cicero with a good omen. Though Neptune had favoured Cicero on his journey, the crows told a more sinister story. They circled him, as he made way for his house and some landed on the windows of his litter pecking at him incessantly, as others cawed ready to devour his flesh.

The assassins, Herennius and Popillius, succeeded in intercepting Cicero's homeward bound litter, and Cicero ordered his servants to set him down. Looking at his would-be murderers he said, 'You have me, I am worn. Do what you will with my outstretched neck.' Herennius plunged his blade into Cicero's chest, penetrating his heart. Herennius chopped off Cicero's head and hands for souvenirs, in accordance with Antonius' request. Cicero's servants terrified by the sight, immediately fled for their own lives.

Whilst Octavianus had agreed to the proscription on Marcus Tullius Cicero, he had done so with grave reluctance. Although Marcus Antonius was a fellow triumvir, he was hardly liked by Octavianus. The triumvirate, for Octavianus, was a political arrangement, not a bond of friendship. Antonius, consumed by jealousy, could not suffer Octavianus' mentor Cicero to live. The head and hands of Cicero were returned to Rome and with much delight Antonius displayed them on the Rosta where orators spoke. The Roman people were horrified and shuddered at the gruesome sight. Many remarked how the face resembled Antonius, rather than that of Cicero.

The bloody proscriptions did not yield the riches and treasure for which the triumvirs had hoped. By 42 BCE the triumvirs were preparing for battle at Phillipi in Greece. Antonius and Octavianus, armed with twenty legions, stood on the hills of Phillipi, jeering at Brutus' and Cassius' forces. The legions slammed on their shields, creating a frightening clamour that could be heard for miles around. Cassius, commanding a much lesser force than Antonius, quivered at the thought of the impending battle. Meanwhile, Brutus stood looking at the forces of Octavianus and assumed that the young general lacked experience. Octavianus trembled as he looked at the forces of Brutus and wondered how he might defeat such an experienced soldier. Antonius, brutal in battle as in life, defeated the legions of Cassius. Cassius, considering the effort futile, committed suicide, yet unknown to him, Brutus had confidently defeated Octavianus and his legions. Despite having a considerable advantage over Octavianus, he did not pursue a second battle for several weeks, which would lead to his downfall. At last, facing the combined forces of Octavianus and Antonius he was finally defeated. With little hope for the future of a republic, Brutus ceremoniously ran a blade through his stomach in much the same way as Cassius had weeks earlier. The perpetual flame of the Vesta shone brightly when Brutus defeated Octavianus, but was nearly extinguished on the day that he committed suicide.

Octavianus, lacked the stomach for further battle wo returned home to Rome shortly after the victory at Phillipi, while Antonius, longing for further victories, embarked on a conquest around Greece and the East. Antonius became ambitious and set about gathering an army so that he might invade Parthia, as Caesar had planned before he was brutally murdered. Early in 41 BCE, Antonius ordered Cleopatra to meet with him in Tarsus, as she was charged with conspiring with Cassius before the battle of Phillipi, or that was what the public thought. Deep within the confines of Antonius' mind, a plot to get Egyptian aide for his Parthian crusade was emerging, but, Cleopatra had an agenda of her own. Cleopatra, well-educated and multi-lingual, seduced Antonius by sailing into Tarsus dressed as the goddess Venus. Venus, knowing the true nature of Cleopatra's intent, was offended at her display. Caesar looked down from the heavens smiling, as he was bemused by the whole affair.

Catering to Antonius' taste for celebrations, the Egyptian seducer soon beguiled him, and it was not long before he followed her back to Alexandria. Whilst Antonius was in love, news of the affair reached Rome, devastating his wife Fulvia. Both Fulvia and Lucius worked hard to maintain Antonius' political connections in Rome against the ever increasing popularity for Octavianus. When Octavianus became aware of the plight, he was enraged but nothing would stop

Antonius from pursuing his exotic Queen. The Parthian crusade had been abandoned in favour of festive occasions and the name 'Fulvia' no longer existed in Antonius' vocabulary.

In 40 BCE, with civil war around the corner, Antonius decided to take responsibility and return to Rome promptly. Antonius' wife, Fulvia, died before he could make it back. When Antonius entered the forum, Octavianus stared at him sternly. 'Have you no time for an old friend?' questioned Antonius upon seeing Octavianus. Octavianus did not budge from his hostile posture with his arms crossed and glowering brows. 'Old friend. Is that what you call it?' stated Octavianus.
'Why of course, my fellow triumvir!' exclaimed Antonius cheerfully.
'Explain, then,' Octavianus said angrily. 'How it is that you have come to neglect your wife and position in Rome for the caresses of some foreign Queen?'

'Dear friend,' Antonius said patronizingly. 'I have not neglected Rome. I am here now, am I not? A man who would not accept his responsibilities would not be here. In regards to Fulvia, she did not satisfy me. Can you not understand that she caused me to stray from her? She is the very reason we are having this conversation and the cause of many problems that have existed between us in the past.'
'Of course, I understand. She was not an easy lady to contend with. Let us put these problems behind us, then.' Octavianus suggested. Antonius nodded in agreement.

After further conversations, both Octavianus and Antonius agreed that they would have designated areas where they had supreme power. Octavianus would have the areas of Italy and Europe whilst Antonius would have Asia, Greece and Egypt. Their pact was then sealed by a marriage alliance between Antonius and Octavianus' sister, Octavia, who was recently widowed. From 40-37 BCE the newly wed couple lived in

Athens and it was there that Octavia had two daughters who were named Antonia. However, Antonius would not stay satisfied with Octavia either, for he would again stray to the sweet caresses of his Asian Queen.

In 37 BCE Antonius finally embarked on his Parthian crusade, meeting up with Cleopatra along the way. Cleopatra had borne Antonius twins after leaving Brundisium. Fully acknowledging his children, he named them Alexander and Cleopatra. Unable to maintain his vows to Octavia, Antonius married Cleopatra according to an Egyptian ceremony, and she later conceived yet another child who would be named Ptolemy. Antonius' mind was so consumed by Cleopatra, that his Parthian campaign failed miserably, costing him in excess of twenty thousand men. Octavia, keen to see her husband, left Rome with gifts and supplies to make way for Athens. Antonius made no effort to stop and meet with her and proceeded immediately to his mistress in Alexandria. When Octavia became aware of this, tears rolled down her cheeks and she questioned how she had failed her husband, but, the failure was not hers, but rather Antonius'.

The sky of Alexandria was clear and the darker blue above the horizon reflected Octavia's mood. Cleopatra, was no stranger to the dark blue sky and the foreboding sun. Ra, the Egyptian sun-god, looked down on Cleopatra and Antonius blessing them both whilst Mars had long since turned his back on the couple, preferred to raise his sword to his Egyptian counterparts. Peace would be short lived, and the couple were unaware of the road that lay ahead of them.

As the years passed, Antonius became increasingly stout from his inactivity and love for feasting. He lacked the fitness and build of the typical Roman general hell bent on conquest. By 32 BCE he donated many of the Eastern territories of Rome to Cleopatra and her children, as he was in love. Antonius declared Caesar's illegitimate son, Caesarion, to be legal heir of Rome and in the same fell swoop Octavia was disgraced by formal divorce. Increasing disgust arose in the streets of Rome over Antonius' actions; especially abandoning Octavia in favour of a foreignQueen. There was a natural distrust of Cleopatra amongst the Roman people, for she was welleducated, foreign, a monarch and, most of all, a woman. According to Roman ideals, women were less educated than men; were subservient to them, and rarely held positions of power unless it was in the Vesta. When the senate came to hear of the news, they swore an extraordinary oath to Octavianus, the true leader of Rome.

Octavianus was certain that war was just around the corner and planned to rally the masses against Antonius in the East. Octavianus was infuriated by the divorce of his sister, so stood on the streets of Rome defaming Antonius' character. Amusing pantomimes were performed in the name of a foreign queen and Roman general. The masked actors acted lewdly when performing Cleopatra, and overtly conceited, when playing Antonius. At around the same time, Plancus and Titus, former supporters of Antonius, returned to Rome, bringing with them the news that anti-Roman and pro-Cleopatra sentiments existed in Antonius' new will. When Octavianus heard of this, he illegally seized the will from safe keeping in the Vesta. The perpetual flame of Rome ignited in fury and the protective virgins of the Vesta stood taken aback by such an action. The senate was also astounded at the action, but Plancus and Titus had supported Octavianus, claiming that they had stood witness to the will. Once the seal was broken, jaws jutted out and brows frowned in displeasure. The contents of the will were read and it declared Caesarion to be the legal heir and their other children to hold claims on Eastern territories. It also indicated that he wished to be buried with Cleopatra in Alexandria. It was not the question of inheritance that most angered Roman citizens, but rather Antonius' denial of Roman funeral rites that most upset them.

Octavianus was convinced that support was dying for Antonius, so encouraged rumours against him. However, he did so carefully, as he was aware that some still favoured his rival triumvir. Octavianus cleverly tricked Antonius' supporters into giving him information whilst claiming that there was no betrayal. This approach won Octavianus' favour, and those who once supported Antonius started to change sides. Roman citizens believed that Antonius was determined to make Cleopatra, Queen of Rome, which won Octavianus further supporters. Octavianus' political genius shone out when he suggested to the senate that Rome should declare war on Cleopatra and Egypt rather than Antonius himself. This political manoeuvre kept Rome safe from the prospect of civil war. As both sides readied themselves for the war, Octavianus received an oath of alliance from Italy and those in the Western provinces, rather than to Rome itself. This was a miracle of sorts, considering that the Roman people disdained the idea of a monarch.

CHAPTER THREE

In Egypt (31 BCE), storm clouds hung in the air, as if signify-
ing the anger of the Roman gods. Mars, god of warfare, readied
himself for battle against the Egyptian deities. Octavianus and
the Senate had declared war on the land of the pharaohs, and an
increasingly overweight Antonius tried on his ill-fitting armour.
In his self-confidence, Antonius expected to have every chance
of winning the war. He was confident that the young Octavianus
had little stomach for fighting, and more time for listless gossip. Queen Cleopatra felt a knot in her stomach and suspected
from the outset that her monarchy was doomed. Though educated in seven languages, she had not been able to negotiate
a truce with Octavianus. The fate was sealed; there was to be
war, and Antonius' soldiers became uneasy with the prospect
of fighting their fellow Romans for the sake of a foreign queen.

Octavianus readied his soldiers in Rome, and made offerings to Neptune, god of the ocean, for this was to be one of
Rome's greatest naval battles. Neptune accepted the sacrifices,
and made sea breezes favour Octavianus' vessels. Both sides
were equally matched, but the morale of Antonius' men was
low, as Cleopatra sailed alongside them in her golden vessel.
Roman women never accompanied their men into battle, but

Cleopatra would not listen to the men's pleas for it to be otherwise. Neptune caused the seas to swell from far beneath the crystal depths of the ocean. One by one, Antonius' vessels were alight from flaming arrows, and soldiers deserted their ships in favour of the sea. Antonius, remaining confident, ordered his remaining cohorts forward, whilst Cleopatra's golden vessel watched the entourage from behind. Each ship that advanced forward was burnt up like the last. Octavianus' legions pelted their shields with their swords, in screams of raucous victory. ple, numerous virgins and eunuchs surounded the perpetual flame, which was burning brightly as ever. The Vestal Virgins were protectors of the flame, and the eunuchs who accompanied them, were the protectors of their virginity. If their chastity.

Seeing the destruction of her navy, Cleopatra turned away and fled in fear of what might happen to her if she were captured. Antonius pressed on until every ship was no more, and found in himself an overwhelming feeling of defeat. He had been dishonoured and outwitted by a youngster who had just proved his ability for battle. Antonius cried out to Mars, asking why he had been forsaken when he was obviously the more experienced soldier. The Egyptian canineheaded god, Anubis, growled viciously at Venus and Neptune, but Apollo, God of Actium, stood proudly in reply, and struck terror into the hearts of the Egyptians. Although a Greek God, Apollo smiled upon Octavianus. He was truly blessed. Antonius should not have lost so easily, for the Egyptians were renowned for their advanced navy. Mars had not accepted Antonius' offerings, but Bacchus, god of mischief and merry-making, had. Every cup of wine that Antonius swilled was a toast to Bacchus. Octavianus' men laughed as they perceived the self-indulgent god riding on the back of a donkey, spilling wine on the decks of the Antonius' ship during the battle.

Octavianus had suspected that Antonius had planned on

invading Italy, so he had blockaded Antonius' fleet whilst it assembled. Octavianus' strategy was to keep war out of Italy and to keep the enemy fleet trapped in the Gulf of Ambracia. The gulf may have seemed like the perfect place to assemble an armada to enter Italy, but Octavianus saw through Antonius' plans. The Gulf was a place of rare beauty, with its salt-flats and crystal clear waters, which cut twenty miles inland. It was a natural haven for an abundance of wildlife. Antonius' camp was set up at the temple of Apollo, with Octavianus' camp further north. Octavianus had advanced down with his men and took over the upper province for his own camp. Stormy weather delayed the battle for days, but on the second of September 31 BCE the weather favoured an attack. The battle was won before the forces met, as Antonius hung back, indecisive and fearful of what might happen. Behind his vessel was a sucking fish, which was renowned for stopping ships in their tracks, so the story is told.

The battle of Actium was over, and Antonius was left with little choice but to retreat like his Egyptian wife. Livy, witness to Octavianus' triumph, etched the following words in his wax tablet:

> Cum M. Antonius ob amorem Cleopatrae, ex qua duos filios habebat, Philadelphum et Alexandrum, neque in urbem venire vallet neque finito IIIviratus empore imperium deponere bellumgue moliretur, quod urbi et Italiae inferret, ingentibus tam navalibus quam terrestribus copiis ob hoc contractis remissoque Octaviae sorori Caesaris repudio, Caesar in Eprium cum exercitu traicit. Pugnae deinde navales et prolia equestria secunda Caesaris referuntur. (Livy, 1959, p. 162).

In English this translates as:

Marcus Antonius, because of his passion for Cleopatra, by

whom he had two sons, Philadelphus and Alexander, was unwilling to return to Rome or to lay down his command when his term of the Board of Three ended; he organised a campaign of invasion against Rome and Italy, and gathered huge forces on sea as well as on land for this purpose, and sent a notice of divorce to Octavia, Caesar's sister. Caesar crossed with an army to Eprius. A description is given of the ensuing naval battles and cavalry engagements, in which Caesar was victorious. (Livy, 1959, p. 163).

It was never suspected that Antonius would enter a death pact with his Egyptian wife, Cleopatra. Between September 31 BCE and July 30 BCE, the defeated husband and wife drank excessively and praised the Egyptian gods of the underworld. Cleopatra took to poisoning convicted felons with all sorts of snakes, and witnessed men die of poisons that were potent and painful. She derived much pleasure from witnessing people die of snake venom, as they convulsed and frothed at the mouth. Her favourite venom was that of an asp, where the victim would be taken by a heavy head and become prone to sleep. Prone to suicide, Cleopatra often fantasised about killing herself with snakes, and she would run the blade of a dagger against her skin, imagining it piercing an artery.

Octavianus, on the other hand, had business in Rome after defeating Antonius at Actium, and, after returning home, closed the gates of Janus, which signalled peace for the first time in two hundred years. He decided that he needed to disband his large army from seventy legions down to twenty-eight, due to its vast cost. His good friend and best general, Agrippa, needed to return to Rome in order to deal with a minor plot by Lepidus' son to take over Rome. When in Rome, he set about acquiring the funds and land for his veterans, who demanded payment after such a long period of service.

Meanwhile, back in Alexandria, Antonius' legions were deserting him in favour of a better life. With no legions defending Alexandria, Octavianus could enter Egypt, but he stayed in Rome awhile to observe the situation. On hearing the news that Octavianus was likely to invade, Antonius decided there was only one option left to him. He went to Cleopatra's bedchamber and, after finding a suicide note, thought that she was dead. The young queen had deceived her lover in the hopes that she would find favour with Octavianus. Tears welled in Antonius' eyes, and he went to an isolated room where no one would disturb him. There he grasped his sword, and fell upon it violently. Proculeius, sent by Octavianus, retrieved the bloodied blade, and took it back to Rome. Upon seeing the sword, Octavianus thought to himself: 'He's actually dead! I can't believe it!' and, with that, he hurried all men away from him. Octavianus sat on a chair in the forum, with his head cupped in his hands. Tears flowed down his face and spilled onto the marble floor of the forum. He lost his composure, and Agrippa walked into the forum. 'What's the matter?' Agrippa asked out of concern for his good friend.

'It's Antonius. He committed suicide this morning', sobbed Octavianus. Agrippa raised his hand to Octavianus' shoulder and told him that this needed to happen in order for him to rule Rome. However, the decisions that had to be made in order to be the sole ruler were contrary to Octavianus' heart-felt wishes. He remembered Octavia's wedding day. She was content, and Antonius seemed like the ideal brother-in-law at first. It had come as a shock when Antonius had divorced Octavia. Despite their differences, Octavianus still respected him, even in death.

Octavianus was mournful for Antonius' fate, but he could not remain so for long, as something needed to be done about the young Egyptian queen. Cleopatra rushed to Caesarion's bedchamber; there she gave her son money, and sent him out of Alexandria into Egypt, scared of what Octavianus might do to him. Meanwhile, Octavianus arrived to converse with Cleopatra. He ordered that all daggers and poison be taken off her person so that she could not commit suicide. Cleopatra, desperate for death, lay on her bed, thinking. She imagined that, if she could manage to seduce the young Octavianus, she would be able to keep her monarchy, as she had done with Antonius. Cleopatra lowered herself in her bed, exposing her naked leg from the sheer smock that she was wearing, and beneath the sheer material the outline of her curvaceous physique could be seen. When Octavianus arrived, she had him sent to her bedchamber, and when he entered the room she fell at his feet, crying and trembling like a young child. He patted her on the head, saying: 'I've come here to comfort you for your loss.' Octavianus took her by the cheek and raised her to her feet. He wiped away her tears and said: 'I too am upset about the situation'. Cleopatra remained silent.

Octavianus made her lie down again, and sat by her bedside. Cleopatra kissed him, and he gently pushed her back in refusal. She began to excuse herself for what she had done, and with a desire to save her empire, she offered Octavianus most of her wealth. But a manservant of Octavianus laughed, and stated that she had more riches than she had alluded to. Cleopatra rose from the bed and attacked the manservant in a fit of anger, boxing him around the ears. Octavianus, bemused by the fray, sat and chuckled as she got angry. Having no more time for the young queen's behaviour Octavianus departed, and set about trying to find Caesarion. He sent out some Egyptian slaves with the message that he wanted to make Caesarion king and to give him all the wealth of Egypt. Before too long the naive teenager came back to Alexandria with visions of immense wealth to come. As soon as Caesarion returned, Octavianus' men killed him. Octavianus also ordered the death of Antonius' elder son Antyllus (to Fulvia), so that there would be no opposition to his rule in Rome. Cleopatra was disgusted at the death of her son, and thought that her two younger children were bound to die, too.

One night, whilst Cleopatra was dining, a countryman came to the gates with a basket full of figs. Octavianus' men inspected the basket and were satisfied with its contents but, at the bottom of the figs, there lay an asp that Cleopatra had ordered. On receiving the basket, the young queen put it in her bedchamber for later and finished dining with Octavianus. After the evening meal, Cleopatra went back to her bedchamber, and took the snake from the basket. She ordered her slaves to take the asp after she had finished with it, then Cleopatra pierced the delicate skin on her arm with the snake's fangs. Slowly her head became heavy and she drifted into a peaceful sleep. Her slaves emulated their mistress and fell into a deep slumber also, except for one slave who convulsed on the floor. Octavianus' men entered and shouted at the half dead slave. 'What has happened here?' they questioned, and she informed them that Cleopatra had poisoned herself.

When Octavianus came to hear of Cleopatra's death, he shook his head and questioned his men: 'How could you let this happen?' Agrippa relayed to Octavianus how the snake had been smuggled in. Octavianus ordered that Cleopatra be buried honourably alongside Antonius. 'Get me Cleopatra's children!' He then exclaimed. Agrippa went to the bedchamber of the two younger children. After telling them that their mother was dead, he sent them to Rome, to be brought up alongside Octavia's children. Octavia enjoyed motherhood, so did not mind raising more children. It was Octavianus' strategy to show mercy to his enemies and their progeny.

Octavianus remained for a year in Egypt, re-establishing the client kingdoms and provinces that had been disrupted by the civil war. Egypt became an imperial province of Octavianus and future Roman Emperors. He returned to Rome in July 29 BCE with all the riches of the Ptolomies, which he dispensed to soldiers and citizens. Octavianus organised a wonderful triple triumph for his victories at Illyricum, Actium and Egypt.

People lined the streets during the celebrations, winessing Octavianus raising his arms up to the crowd. Soldiers were praised for their victories, and the war-weary men were pleased to lower their shields in the name of peace. The Ptolomies' wealth was distributed evenly between the military and citizens of Rome. Everyone partook of a sumptuous banquet, and the impoverished were grateful to Octavianus for the corn dole, a socialist privilege, which dealt with mass unemployment brought in by the Gracchi brothers, a hundred years earlier. Agrippa reflected proudly on his accomplishments and sensed that his career as a general was just as successful as his achievements in architecture and infrastructure. Cleopatra's children settled into their new home with Octavia; there they learnt Greek and Latin, an education that most patricians would have had. Antonius' deserters were welcomed with open arms, feeling disillusioned by their former general's actions and failures.

Octavianus knew, that if he resigned his power over the army, civil war might recur. If he retained power as an autocrat over his army and the state, he might end up assassinated like his adoptive father Iulius Caesar. Octavianus was unable to disband his army, as this would leave the borders of the vast state open to attack. To solve his problem, Octavianus proceeded with great caution, and maintained his office of consul for the first few years. Holding office as consul would ensure he held power in the traditional way, which would make him less of a target for assassination. He sought to re-establish business confidence, so he cancelled debts owing to the state, and henceforth the interest rates fell by two thirds.

The members of the Senate gathered together to listen to Octavianus' proposal. The old men surrounded the consul. Their eyes were fixed on the consular figure, as the head of Senate called out: 'Convening for laws promulgated during the civil war'. The first man stood up and said: 'I call for the laws promulgated during the war to be annulled as they were unjust'. The head of the senate asked for all those in favour. For a moment no one raised their hand, as they were waiting for Octavianus to address the Senate. Octavianus sat for a while, put his clammy hands together, and then moved to the centre of the Senate House and addressed the senators: 'I, Gaius Iulius Caesar Octavianus, call for the aforementioned laws promulgated to be annulled'. The crowd cheered and, with that, Octavianus was seated in the consular chair. The head of the Senate called for those in favour, and every single hand went up out of fear of what Octavianus might do if they disapproved. The motion was carried, and this worked in Octavianus' favour, as Romans had seen enough civil war.

As Octavianus reduced his army from seventy legions to twenty-eight, his men became demanding, wanting their land allotments delivered to them. Octavianus picked the men that had been in ten years of service or more to retire first. One hundred thousand men stood before Octavianus, cheering, and he addressed them all with a memorable speech. Octavianus stood outside the Forum and addressed his men: 'Citizens and Veterans of Rome, you have indeed worked hard for this day. You fought alongside me to defeat Pompey and Antonius. You have been beaten and bruised by harsh weather, but your bodies stood the test. Barbarians attacked you, yet you shook them off. You have fought bravely. You respected and obeyed your General. You have seen the spoils of war and seen countless friends die. Yet you, every one of you, stood strong and fought until the end. We have conquered countless territories together, and this is where you will find your new homes. Go forth and take your land allotments in Italy, Carthage and Syria. Go home to your wives and make love to them liberally. Take your gold to your sons and tell them that all your wealth will be theirs one day. But know this, Gaius Iulius Caesar Octavianus has blessed you with your wealth and land. Go home free and farm your crops.' One hundred thousand men roared with excitement, and they drank wine and gambled into the night.

Just a year later, in 28 BCE, Octavianus and his consular colleague Agrippa held a census. Meanwhile, in the Senate House, men were jeering at Octavianus. One part of the moderate faction stood up. 'We cannot be subject to Caesar's will. If he has it his way, there will be no Senate left'. This was not Octavianus' plan; it was merely to reduce the number of senators to a more manageable size. As Agrippa and Octavianus entered the Senate house, the squabbling old men fell quiet. Their jaws jutted out and on their faces were expressions of extreme displeasure. 'Gentlemen!' Octavianus called, before the men resumed quarrelling amongst themselves. 'Gentlemen, may I have your attention please?' Octavianus pleaded. 'It is not my intention to throw out experienced members of the Senate. It is just that we have so many senators that there is disorder every time the Senate house is full. This house can only hold eight hundred people at the maximum. We have to do something. First, I call for voluntary resignations.' The leader of the Senate called out: 'All those in favour of resignation' and a few hundred hands went up. Octavianus moved to the middle of the Senate house and said: 'Gentlemen, that's a start, but we still need to cull another two hundred. All those in favour of voluntary resignation, please leave,' and some did so. 'Now what I propose is that we retire anyone aged above seventy' and, with that, another fifty left. 'With the remainder, we will cast votes on individuals and those eight hundred with the highest votes will stay and the others will leave'. After going through a gruelling census, the number was cut down to eight hundred senators. Octavianus' name headed the Senatorial list and his title now became 'Princeps Senatus'.

In Octavianus' seventh consulship, he encountered Lucinius Crassus, who had earned military accolades in Thrace and Macedonia. Lucinius was the grandson of the first triumvir, Crassus, who was consul in 70 and 55 BCE. The two men had met at a social occasion at Octavia's house. The house was adorned with the usual paintings of the family tree in the loungearea. People lay on their sides on marble seats eating rich grapes and exotic fruit. Octavia, a good hostess, brought in a pig on the spit, over which her slaves had toiled for hours. The embers beneath the pig warmed the large lounge room, and the smell of pork wafted in the air, making people hungry.

As people were carving up the pig, Octavianus went to meet the young Lucinius Crassus. The two of them talked for a while about his military feats; Octavianus became uneasy, and left the conversation. He addressed Agrippa, his good friend and advisor: 'Agrippa, Lucinius Crassus' military exploits are very threatening.'
'In what way?' Agrippa questioned.
'Well,' he said, pausing. 'Since I have reduced my military forces from seventy to twenty-eight legions, I'm in a weaker position. With Crassus earning military accolades in Thrace and Macedonia, what is to stop him from challenging my political power?'
Agrippa nodded and said: 'That is a problem. I don't think he has that personal ambition, though, look at how meek he is with everyone about his triumphs.'
'We both know politics; people will present things differently as a means to an end.'
'But really, I repeat that I don't think that he has that personal ambition, Octavianus. Cornelius Gallus over there is a threat.'
Octavianus nodded. He mused about Cornelius only a moment before deciding that he didn't like the man very much. Cornelius laughed with his friends and glanced sideways at Octavianus. He came up to Octavianus and said that he was glad to see him, but Octavianus did not engage him in conversation, as he was certain that Cornelius was too ambitious for his own good. After assessing his rivals at Octavia's feast, Octavianus appeared before the Senate house once again, to skilfully apply one of his political manoeuvres. The date was the 13th of January 27 BCE, and dismay was felt throughout Rome when Octavianus gave up all of his powers and provinces to the Senate and the people. 'I shall bestow my powers upon the Republic so as not

to be mistaken for a tyrant,' he stated in a proud gesture before the aging men of Rome. The action was met with disapproving eyes, for these men had entrusted the Republic to this skilful young orator and general. Agrippa smiled and nudged Octavianus to explain himself further. 'If the Senate should feel that I am the protector of Rome, and were to bestow these honours upon me, I would make it my duty to help the Republic with her cause'. An aging man by the name of Metellus stood before Octavianus and spoke: 'As representative of the Senate and People of Rome, I implore you to take proconsular imperium over Gaul, Spain and Syria for a period of ten years'. By taking on proconsular imperium over the aforementioned provinces, Octavianus offered himself for the position of consul in the years, 26, 25, 24, 23, 5 and 2 BCE. No man hadever held consulship for as long as Octavianus, and he proved to be the longest serving consul, holding power for a period of thirteen years, a precedent set by Caius Marius in earlier years of the Late Republic.

As time passed, the Senate bestowed many honours upon Octavianus. Among them was a golden shield, proclaiming his valour, clemency, and justice. A door post decorated with oak and laurel was presented to him, and, most importantly, he had the name Augustus bestowed upon him. This name does not have a literal translation in English, but it did serve as a station given to those who had been commended by the gods, as well as men. Venus, grandmother of Iulius Caesar, looked down on the newly transformed Augustus and approved of his station. Iulius Caesar, demigod to the people of Rome, was likewise proud of his adoptive son's successes. The Senate renamed the month Sextilis to August, and that name has remained to this day. From this time, Augustus was known as 'Princeps' (First Citizen of Rome), and his regime as the 'Principate'. This period of time became known to later generations as the 'First Settlement'. Augustus effectively concentrated his military power by controlling the provinces with the most legions (twenty in total), whilst the Senate was weakened by only controlling six. After the First Settlement of 27 BCE, Augustus left Rome on his black horse with a small band of men. Agrippa and Taurus, good friends of Augustus, were left in Rome to serve as consuls whilst campaigns against the Cantabrian tribe were underway in the Western Provinces. Augustus and his men camped on the roadside outside Rome; there they feasted until the early hours of the morning. Two men, Magnus and Marius, spoke with Augustus on the need for a Second Settlement in Rome. Magnus was a skilful listener and quiet man; his stubble and shoulder length hair hid the expressive lines in his face. Marius was more talkative, full of new ideas he wanted to share, but when Magnus spoke, his words were that of a wise man who had listened carefully to the conversation, and had assessed the validity of various statements. 'Magnus,' called Augustus. 'Do you think that it is wise to give up the position of consul, so that other Senators might take on the station?' Magnus nodded in acknowledgement, and stated that it would free Augustus from routine affairs as consul so that he might aim for more powerful positions.

After returning to Rome, Augustus called by the Senate once again, and had the lapdog senators vote him in as 'Marius Imperium Proconsulare', in order that his imperium would be the greatest power, superseding the powers of other proconsuls. The period was extended for ten years, and allowed him to enter the Pomerium, the sacred boundaries of the city, without relinquishing such a power. Soon after, Augustus obtained the position of 'Tribunicia Potestas', which enabled him to have the power of the tribunes, thus allowing laws to be passed through without objection. Magnus looked across through his shoulder length hair at Augustus and addressed everyone present: 'The settlements made will ensure that the power of the principate rests on two things, "The Marius Imperium Pronconsulare" and the "Tribunicia Potestas." This will effectively allow Augustus to supersede all authority to command and give him the advantage of promulgating new laws.'

Augustus nodded. Marius spoke up and said that he had already thought of that, wanting to take the credit for Magnus' observation. Magnus called him a docile lupine and smirked. Although Augustus skilfully manoeuvred himself under the banner of the Republic, but in reality he was a clever autocrat.

Augustus finished with the men at the Senate house, and sat outside on the stairs of the Forum. He thought about his lovely wife, Livia, and how happy he was when his daughter Iulia was born to his earlier wife, Scribonia. He would have been happier had he a son, but a daughter could be married off to cement political alliances. Marriages were not about love in ancient Rome, though it did seem that there must have been a bond between Augustus and Livia, as their marriage outlasted most of the other aristocratic unions. Augustus' lack of a son would cause difficulty later on when he was looking for a successor, as the union between Augustus and Livia never bore children. It was often said that Livia was the great woman behind Augustus, and influenced him on a number of decisions, although her voice was not publically heard. Livia, like most wives, waited at home for her husband's return, wondering what had happened over the course of the day.

CHAPTER FOUR

The planets, namesakes of the gods, Jupiter, Mars and Venus, were in perfect alignment in September 63 BCE, and Atia's screams were heard by the heavens. A baby boy, said by learned Greeks to be the son of Apollo, was born in Rome to Atia. Her labour had been long and arduous, but, despite the pain, she could not contain her joy when she heard the child was a boy. In the heavens, there had been great omens, and, according to astrologers, this baby would one day bring peace to Rome. His father, Caius Octavius, raised his son in his arms to acknowledge the would-be heir to his fortune, a ritual known to the Romans as 'sublatus'. Nine days after the birth, the infant was given his father's name, Caius Octavius, on 'dies lustricus', the day of purification. No one, except for Jupiter, Mars and Venus, knew that this child was destined to become the heir of Iulius Caesar, finally having the honour of the title Augustus being bestowed upon him. Despite the child's sickly nature, he would live to an old age, and marry twice in his lifetime. The young Octavius had two sisters, Octavia Major, and Octavia Minor. It is Octavia Minor, his full-blood sister, with whom people are familiar. Octavia Major, his half-sister, and several years his senior, was the daughter of his father's previous wife, Ancharia.

In his old age, Augustus struggled to remember his father, who died when he was just four years old. Atia, Augustus' mother, had been widowed early in his life, although he remembered her telling him that his father and she had been married in 65 BCE, just a couple of years before his birth. Because of her connections to Iulius Caesar, Atia needed the permission of her uncle to marry Octavius. Augustus' father had been a well-off equite (merchant class), whereas his mother was a patrician (upper class). These sorts of mixed marriages were common, as the equites brought wealth, and patricians brought valuable political alliances to the union. The father figure that Augustus did remember was L. Marcius Philppus, who married his mother in the spring of 57 BCE. Although it was common for young males to be educated by their fathers after the age of six, Augustus received his education from his mother in his formative years. One day Augustus was learning to write Greek, and his mother screamed at him. 'Octavius, that use of grammar is poor, and will not endear you to other statesmen. My son will speak perfectly in Greek with a neutral accent, and his literacy will reflect his well-spoken manner. I have visions of your greatness, and the omens show that you will conquer the world one day.' The young Octavius rolled his eyes, and set about correcting hls grammar in his wax tablet. Had it not been for his maternal line, and persistent mother, he never would have become the heir to Caesar's legacy.

Generations later, Suetonius wrote a biography on Augustus; having access to valuable primary evidence, he etched down the following:

Decendens Macedonia, prius quam profiteri se candidtum consulates posset, mortem obiitt repentinam, superstitibus liberis Octavia maiore, quam ex Ancharia, et Octavia minore item Augusto, quos Atia tulerat. Atia M. Atio Balbo et Iulia, sorore C. Caesaris, gentia est. Balbus paterna stripe Aricinus, multis in familia senatoriis imaginibus, a matre Magnum Pompeium artissimo con-

tingebat gradu, functusque honore praeturae inter vigin-
tiviros agrum Campanum plebe Iulia lege divisit. Verum
idem Atonius, despiciens etiam maternam Augusti origi-
nem, proavum eius Afri generis fuisse et modo unguen-
tariam tabernam modo pistrinum Ariciae exercuisse
obicit. Cassius quidem Parmensis quadam epistula non
tantum ut pistoris, sed etiam ut numnulari nepotem sic
taxat Augustum: "Materna tibi farina est ex crudissimo
Ariciae pistrino; hane finxit minibus collybo decloratis
Nerulonenesis mensarius." (Suetonius, 1951, p. 126).

In English this translates as:
While returning home from Macedonia, before he [Au-
gustus' father] could declare himself a candidate for the
consulship, he died suddenly, survived by three children,
an elder Octavia by Ancharia, and by Atia a younger Octavia and Augustus. Atia was the daughter of Marcus Atius Balbus and [Iulia], sister of [Caius] Caesar. Bulbus, a
native of Aricia on his father's side, and of a family dis-
playing many senatorial portraits, was closely connected
on his mother's side with Pompey the Great...But Antonius again, trying to disparage the maternal ancestors of
Augustus as well, twits him with having a great-grand-
father of African birth, who kept a perfumery shop and
then a bakery at Aricia. Cassius of Parma also taunts Augustus with being the grandson both of a baker and of a
money-changer, saying in one of his letters: "Your mother's meal came from a vulgar bakeshop of Aricia; this a
money-changer from Nerulum kneaded into shape with
hands stained with filthy lucre." (Suetonius, 1951, p. 127).

Every June, Atia and Octavia Major prepared for the festival Vestalia, which was celebrated in honour of Vesta, the sacred goddess of the hearth. At the age of eleven, on the ninth of
June, Octavia Minor got the ass from the stable, and started to
decorate it with garlands of violets and strings of small loaves.

Octavius questioned his sister: 'What on earth are you doing?' Octavia Minor answered in a snappy voice: 'You don't pay much attention to your sisters or what they do, do you? It's for the festival of Vestalia. Have you forgotten that the ass is given a holiday on the ninth of June and paraded up and down the street?' Octavius smirked and poked his tongue at his sister, gesturing rudely. 'I don't pay attention to women's affairs, I have better things to do, like perfecting my Greek', he stated. Octavia Major entered the stable, and commented that their mother would be pleased with her younger sister's efforts to honour the goddess, Vesta. 'Octavia, Octavius is being obnoxious', cried Octavia Minor. Some years older than her younger siblings, Octavia Major was more mature about the situation. Now pregnant with a child of her own, she had no time for such sibling rivalry.

From the period of the seventh to the fifteenth of June, all public business ceased, so that matrons like Atia and Octavia Major could make offerings to the goddess. Octavia Major gathered her younger siblings together and told both of them a story about the Temple of the Vesta. She stated: 'The temple of the Vesta is the symbol for the house of the hearth of ancient kings. The 'Rex Sarcrorum' is the king and the vestal virgins his daughters, which total in the number of six.' 'Why does the number of girls total six? Mother said it used to be four.' Octavia Minor pointed out. 'That is true enough, Octavia, but I do not know why it is now six in number,' Octavia Major commented. 'Can I become a Vestal Virgin?' Octavia Minor asked. Octavius shook his head and explained that she was too old to become one. He explained that she was born of both equite and patrician blood so would not qualify to be a Vestal. According to Octavius, she needed to be of noble birth. 'How long does a Vestal serve for?' Octavia Minor questioned. Octavius went on to explain that the Vestal Virgin would need to serve for a period of thirty years whereby she would spend the first ten years of her life training to be one, the next ten years serving as one, and the last ten years teaching others to become one.

Years later, in July 43 BCE, Octavianus, later to be Augustus, marched on Rome, but, before he did so, he made sure that both his sister and mother were safe. Atia and Octavia Minor took refuge in the Temple of the Vesta to ensure that the Senate or others did not harm them. It was possible, if given the chance, that people would have set out to target the women, as a way of getting to Octavianus. One of Atia's slaves brought word to Octavianus that both ladies were in hiding, and were out of public view. Whilst in the Temple of the Vesta, Atia made sacrifices to ensure Octavianus' success and, sure enough, things turned to his advantage, with him being legally declared as Iulius Caesar's heir. If it had not been for the strict laws and customs surrounding the Temple of the Vesta, Atia and Octavia would not have been safe. The Vestals' vocation was to protect the perpetual flame of Rome, ensuring that it never went out, except for when it was renewed on the first of March every year. Important wills, such as Caesar's and Antonius', were kept in the Vesta for protection, and when the subject died a Vestal would take it to the Senate to be read.

At the age of nineteen, Octavianus was voted in as consul for the first time, and his kinsman Q. Pedius was his consular colleague. Pedius was not Octavianus' first choice, as he was betrothed to Servillia, daughter of Publius Servilius Isauricus, and he most certainly would have preferred the election of his soon-to-be father-in-law. Suddenly, between the period of the nineteenth of August and the seventeenth of November 43 BCE, Atia became mortally ill. Octavia stayed by her mother's side, and tried desperately to nurse her back to health. 'Mother,' Octavia whispered. 'Shall I get Octavianus to come home and see you?' As she nodded, tears flowed down her cheek from the pain. When Octavianus returned to see his mother, he was shocked at her condition. He looked at Octavia and said: 'It was being in hiding and the stress of being anonymous amidst the Vestal virgins that has contributed to her ill health'. Octavia continued nursing her mother a while, whilst Octavianus sat in his chair tapping his fingers together. He rose from his seat, and beckoned his sister to him. 'Octavia, I cannot allow my grief for mother to get in the way of what I am to do next. Please understand that I care, but upon her death I will no longer be answerable to anyone except myself. This will give me a distinct political advantage.' Octavia slapped him across the face, and Octavianus raised his hand to his stinging cheek. 'You could at least say that you lost everything that mattered to you,' she spat. 'First, our father, uncle Iulius, and now our mother.' Though disapproving of Octavia's opinion, he let the statement go for the sake of peace. Atia was given a formal public funeral with honours upon Octavianus' request.

Romans lived in the anticipation of death, due to various childhood diseases, or dying in childbirth, or for many other reasons. Atia's corpse was displayed in public on a chariot, and was followed by a procession of people wearing death masks of her deceased distinguished relatives, Iulius Caesar amongst them. The funeral made its way to the Forum, and the masked representations of Atia's ancestors sat on specially prepared thrones. Atia's life was praised, along with Iulius Caesar's. Octavianus addressed his relatives and friends: 'Ladies and gentlemen, it is on this day that I speak of my mother's passing. Atia, from the distinguished line of the Iulii, was both a good mother and wife. She saw that all her children received the best education possible.' People like Agrippa, who knew her well, mourned her death and showed their respects at the funeral. Tears poured from Octavia's eyes as she placed the torch beneath her mother's body, and soon the flames engulfed her remains. After the funeral there was a purification period, which allowed for bereaved family members to be excused from public functions, but when nine days passed, the mourning period ended, and Octavianus returned to public affairs.

Before Atia's death, Octavianus broke off his existing engagement to Servillia in favour of a betrothal to Clodia, Antonius' step-daughter, for political alliances related to the triumvirate. Octavianus was careful about entering a marriage with Clodia, maintaining that she was too young. As the triumvirate disintegrated, so too did promises of marriage to Clodia. In 43 BCE, Octavianus instead made the commitment of marriage to Scribonia, who was to mother his only daughter Iulia (39BCE). In his later years, Augustus brought in legislation regarding a child's birth, the 'lex Aelia Sentia' and the 'lex Papia Poppaea'. It was compulsory for citizens to register a birth within thirty days, and the procedure could be performed by the father, grandfather or the mother at the 'Aerarium Saturni' in Rome. Birth records were collected, officially noted down on papyri and, much like modern times, a birth certificate was obtained with the signature of seven witnesses. A child's birth record was very accurate indeed, including the day, month and hour a child was born. The birthday of a family member had great religious significance to Romans. Birthdays were an excuse for citizens to be festive, and in the house there would be an altar made out of earth. Offerings were given to the Genius, if the person was a male, and Juno, if the person was a female, with candles being lit and incense burnt. Everyone who arrived at the birthday party wore white, and a dinner was made for guests who were invited. The age old tradition of bearing gifts as a guest was commonplace.

In her youth, Iulia played knuckle bones and flipped coins, calling out: 'Heads or Ships?' The tradition of flipping coins passed down through the generations, a piece of Roman history that has been preserved. Iulia loved to play a dice game called 'Par, Impar' (Odds and Evens), and like most children, kept a pet, hers being a parrot by the name of Jupiter. Iulia's wild imagination led her into all sorts of mischief, and one day, as an adult, she would be disgraced for scandalous behaviour.

Iulia was twelve, when her father became known by the

name Augustus. Some sources state that Iulia was taken from her mother Scribonia, and then raised by Augustus and his second wife, Livia. Other stories say that she grew up with her mother. Given the usual practices, she was most likely taken from Scribonia, and brought up in Augustus' household. When Iulia became old enough, she went to live with her step-mother Livia, and was educated to be a lady of high standing. Livia was a strict woman, who was very old-fashioned when it came to educating youngsters. In addition to her studies in the Greek classics, Iulia learnt womanly duties, such as weaving and spinning. She took a keen interest in poetry, literature and high culture, something that was common in the Augustan household. Augustus maintained strict control of Iulia's social circle, and she could only see those who had been approved by him, a trait that he had inherited from his beloved mother. Because Augustus had a deep affection for his daughter, he made sure she had the best teachers available. Once, whilst talking with his friends, he made a remark about his daughter: 'Two capricious daughters have I tolerated: Rome and Iulia'

Whilst procreation was the main reason for marriage at that time and place, there were many childless unions that were happy ones. Although Augustus had a daughter from a previous marriage with Scribonia, he was nonetheless in love with his second wife, Livia, even though they had produced no children of their own. Augustus brought in a moral legislation for childless women between the ages of twenty and fifty who were divorced or widowed. The legislation stated that such a woman would need to remarry within two years if she was widowed, and eighteen months if she were divorced. In the case where children had fathers, but the mother was deceased or divorced, those progeny would be raised by the paternal side of the family. A man might remarry, and the children would be subject to a step-mother. Alternatively, he might decide to take a concubine, so that the children would avoid having a step family. When Livia divorced her husband in favour of Augustus, her son Tiberius was raised by his father.

Scribonia, mother of Iulia, was said to be a disagreeable woman,according to Suetonius. She was markedly older than Octavianus, and had had children from previous marriages. Scribonia was the younger sister of Pompeian Scribonius Libo, who was born around 90 BCE. Libo was not important, but his family connections to Sextus Pompeius, the younger son of Popey, were. Sextus Pompeius had control of Sicily, and was in a position to starve Italy of essential grain supplies, hence the reason for this marriage alliance. It was surmised that Scribonia, Libo's younger sister, was close to him in age, but it now appears that there might have been an age gap of twenty years between the two of them. Sources indicate that she might have actually been the daughter of Libo, rather than his sister, but this is hard to discern, as her name would have been identical with either family connection. The exact age of Scribonia is shrouded in mystery; as far as one can tell she would have been at least thirty, if not older, when she married Augustus. When they married, Octavianus was only twentythree, and, as mentioned earlier, had been betrothed twice. Despite the betrothals, Octavianus was inexperienced with marriage, and the political implications of the marriage alliance were not the only things to hold it together, as there was also the expectation that they would produce heirs. The marriage between them only lasted a year, and in 39 BCE, Sextus Pompeius' admiral abandoned him, giving up the provinces of Sardinia and Corsica. According to Antonius, Augustus divorced Scribonia for her outspoken nature in relation to Livia. It was said that Scribonia showed a strong character when Iulia was sent into exile; she too moved from Rome, and went to lend her support to her daughter. It was Scribonia's choice to support her daughter, and modern generations have interpreted this as her being involved in the scandal that caused Iulia's exile, but it is likely that both mother and daughter shared similar opinions of Augustus.

During his unhappy marriage, Octavianus fell deeply in love with Livia, and the two were married on the seventeenth of January 38 BCE. Livia was born on the thirtieth of January 59 or 58 BCE. Suetonius explains that the couple met when they were both married. Livia was six months' pregnant when she divorced her husband, and Scribonia was said to have been divorced on the very day she gave birth to Iulia. Tiberius C. Nero and Livia divorced on mutual grounds. He was present at the wedding and gave her away to Augustus, as though he was her father. The importance of the Claudii family, with whom Livia was connected, may have been another reason for their union. Despite being a woan, Octavianus gave Livia the freedom to control her own finances in 35 BCE, which was rarely done. Octavianus had a public statue dedicated to Livia, and she formed the role model for Roman women. Livia lived modestly in their house on Palatine Hill, despite having considerable wealth and power. She neither adorned herself in expensive jewelry nor exotic scents, for the couple had a reputation of meekness to uphold. She took to involving herself in conversations with Octavianus about politics, and on numerous occasions she influenced his opinions.

One night, whilst in his home at Palatine Hill, Augutus had a conversation with his wife. Livia had cooked up a sumptuous feast for her husband, and together they sat at the table. Augustus bit into a piece of bread, and whilst chewing he asked: 'What factors do you think are important to a successful Principate?' Livia paused, thought for a while, and then answered. 'Well, there should be eight factors to a successful Principate. Character, approach, circumstance, religion, literature, politics and military.' She went on to explain that Augustus' character had demonstrated a single-minded determination to achieve what no other could before. Livia told him that he had been ruthless with the proscriptions when he needed to be, and that he had a clear purpose, using the appropriate people with the appropriate skills to do what he couldn't. 'Just look at your approach towards the situation,' she stated, pouring him a wine. 'You used the wide ranging powers granted to you, such as those accorded to you as tribune. Your circumstance is that you are Caesar's heir, and in having this title you became loved by the people. You also fed and entertained angry mobs, which has contributed to internal stability. With religion, you had your father, Iulius Caesar, deified, which has helped you maintain political control, but if I might add, I think that you are not devoting enough time to the literate side of society. Approach the writers. There are Horace, Virgil and Livy to be dealt with.' Then she elaborated on his political and military position. Augustus raised his eyebrows in surprise, as his wife outlined the most important principals of the Principate.

Livia proved to be equal in ambition to her husband, and although she was not directly involved in politics, she pushed her sons towards powerful positions. Drusus, her youngest son, was a trusted general, and was married to Augustus' most favoured niece, Antonia Minor. Livia influenced Augustus in taking her son, Tiberius, to marry Iulia in 11 BCE, and named him as his heir in 4 CE. Rumours spread that Livia had been responsible for Marcellus' (Augustus' nephew) death. Iulia's two sons to Marcus Agrippa were adopted by Augustus as heirs initially, and, according to the story, Livia had them poisoned. The only remaining son in Augustus' family, Agrippa Postumus, was arrested, incarcerated and killed, which left his step-son Tiberius to fill his place. Many say that it was too convenient that all possible male heirs of Augustus' bloodline had died. Livia's ultimate intent was to make life difficult for her step-daughter, and in doing so she completely ruined her family.

In 37 BCE, Augustus' friends, Caius Maecenas and Marcus V. Agrippa, suggested that he arrange a betrothal between his daughter, aged two, and Marcus Antonius' son, Antyllus, aged ten. Iulia's betrothal to Antyllus never led to marriage, as Antonius was defeated in the Battle of Actium. Like many Roman women, Iulia focused on marrying well, and producing political alliances. In 25 BCE, at the tender age of fourteen, she married her cousin Marcus C. Marcellus, who was only three years older. It was assumed by some that Augustus had chosen Marcellus as a possible heir, but this was unlikely, as Augustus was fighting a war in Spain. Agrippa was entrusted with looking after Iulia's marriage in Augustus' absence. When Iulia was sixteen she was widowed, and her first marriage had produced no heirs.

By 21 BCE, now aged eighteen, Iulia married Agrippa, who was from a modest family, but had earned a title with Augustus. This political alliance was advised by his friend, Maecenas, who commented that Augustus made Agrippa so great that he should be his son-in-law or be put to death. Agrippa was twenty-five years Iulia's senior, and their marriage was arranged to present a political advantage to Augustus. Iulia, unhappy in this union, had no connection to her husband, so she fell in love with a younger man, by the name of Sempronius Gracchus, with whom she had an affair. Iulia became known for her adulterous ways, and according to Suetonius, she also fell in love with her stepbrother Tiberius during her marriage to Agrippa. The couple lived in a villa near Farnesina in Trastevere. Their marriage, though unhappy, was a fruitful one, and resulted in five children by the following names: Caius Caesar, Vipsania Iulia, Lucius Caesar, Vipsania Agrippina Major and Agrippa Postumus. Agrippa was governor of Gaul, and it is likely that Iulia followed him to his station. Not long after they arrived in Gaul, she gave birth to their first son, and in 19 BCE she gave birth to a girl. After returning to Rome, their third child, a son, was born. Whilst married to Agrippa, Iulia made way to where her husband was campaigning, but she was caught in a flood around Troy, and almost drowned. Agrippa fined the locals in a fury, but no one was brave enough to challenge him. Herod, King of Judaea, met with Agrippa to arrange a pardon, and it was only then that he removed the fine. The couple made their way through the eastern provinces, and visited Herod in his home town. In 14 BCE, their fourth child, a baby girl, was born in Athens. Augustus was responsible for the children's education, and in 17 BCE he adopted the two boys, Lucius and Caius Caesar, both under the age of three. When the family returned to Italy, Iulia became pregnant again, but this time her husband died suddenly, aged fifty-one. Augustus was gravely saddened by the death of his good friend, Agrippa, and decided that he should be buried in the mausoleum alongside his other relatives.

After the death of Agrippa, Iulia was married off to Tiberius, her stepbrother, for the sake of Augustus' dynastic interests. In order for Tiberius to marry Iulia, he had to divorce his beloved wife Agrippina, daughter to another wife of Agrippa. The marriage was doomed, and the son that Iulia bore Tiberius died in infancy. According to Suetonius, Tiberius did not think highly of his wife's character, and it was most certainly clear from other sources that she now disdained Tiberius. It was said in some sources that Iulia sent her father a letter speaking ill of her husband. By 6 BCE, the couple had separated. In 2 BCE, Iulia was arrested for adultery and treason. Augustus had sent her a letter in Tiberius' name, declaring that the marriage was null and void. Tiberius, paranoid of Iulia, remarked that she had plotted to kill him. At the time, whilst Augustus was bringing in legislation for family values, his daughter was accused of having affairs with other men. He could not allow this to set an example to Roman women, so Iulia was exiled, along with her supposed lovers. Iulia was sent to a small Island in harsh conditions, and was not allowed to have any visitors unless her father gave permission. Five years passed before Iulia was allowed back to the mainland.

Augustus spoke with his wife Livia, and told her that he was saddened by Iulia's behaviour. Lucius and Caius, his adopted sons, had both died; leaving him without an heir. Livia's youngest son had also died, which left Augustus with the greatest question: 'Who will succeed me when I am gone?'. Tiberius seemed to be the only candidate, although Augustus had desperately tried to get one of his own bloodline to succeed him. With Augustus getting older, he needed to prepare the next emperor for his duties, and, in the remaining years of his life, he wrote the 'Res Gestae Divi Augusti', which was an autobiographical record of the achievements of the Divine Augustus. Livia quietly suggested that Augustus' choices were limited, and that her son, Tiberius, would make a good heir.

CHAPTER FIVE

Both Lucius and Caius, legal heirs to Augustus, passed away in their youth, which left the emperor with no choice but to adopt his step-son Tiberius. Tiberius thanked the gods for his blessings, and assumed the powers that had been bestowed on his step-father, so that he could rule alongside him in his senior years. In his early years, Augustus had written the account of his achievements, which would become known as the Res Gestae Divi Augusti. Livia had often questioned why he started writing his autobiography so early on in his life. Augustus stated: 'I am a mortal man, and have been blessed with good fortune from the gods, but not good health. Any number of diseases could infect me and take my life, so with this in mind I must live in anticipation of death'. These factors caused the emperor to prepare every detail of his funeral, and start building his burial site, before he went to war with Antonius in 32 BCE. Stone masons throughout Rome worked hard on the mausoleum, which would become the final resting place for Augustus' family members. Situated outside the sacred perimeter of the city, the site would become known as one of the places where Roman custom was most respected. It showed that Augustus, unlike traitors such as Antonius, had wanted his remains to be kept in his homeland. Antonius, on the other hand, wanted to be buried alongside his Egyptian mistress, which showed no loyalty to Rome. By 28 BCE, all of Augustus' rivals had been defeated or killed, and the mausoleum became the representation of the greatness of the principate. This structure was unmatched in size, stood one hundred and fifty feet tall with a diameter of almost two hundred and ninety feet. The walls of the mausoleum were rendered in white marble, which glistened in the sunlight.

This mega-structure became the tomb of Marcellus, first husband of Julia, and housed the ashes of Marcus Agrippa, Caius and Lucius Caesar. Augustus instructed his men to carve inscriptions of the dead into the marble facing. Bit by bit, the masons chipped away the marble, and word by word an account of each man's achievements was formed. 'When I die, two bronze pillars will contain my last words,' stated Augustus. After his death these pillars were put at the front entrance of the mausoleum for all to read. Surrounding the building was a well cared-for garden, which possessed many flowering shrubs. A well-manicured hedge led out from the entrance, and statues of the gods could be seen throughout the gardens. Open parks welcomed the families of Roman citizens, allowing for respect to be paid to this great leader. A young plebeian boy wandered through the gardens and stood in awe of the trophies that surrounded the structure. He approached the 'Ara Pacis Augusti' (Augustus' peace altar), which had been constructed after the emperor had returned from Gaul in 13 BCE. Later, in the southern district of the mausoleum, the youngster hopped on a stone monument with bronze lines, which indicated the day, month, year and hour. The shadow from the enormous indicator covered the boy, and fell on the hour marked 'IV'. The indicator was covered in hieroglyphics, and had obviously been brought back from the land of the Pharaohs. The boy imagined what the symbols might mean, and decided that it was writing from the gods, as he had never seen anything quite like it. He interpreted one hieroglyphic to mean that the gods were watching his every move, as the picture was representative of a gigantic eye. The child screamed in terror: 'Mamma, Mamma, the gods are after me. They are watching me and blocking out the sun.' His mother took him from the middle of the sundial, and explained that this monument was designed to tell people the time, month and year. She calmed down the child, and said, 'The shadow is designed to fall on that monument there'. She pointed to the Ara Pacis Augusti. 'When the shadow covers that, we know it is a seasonal equinox, which means that the day is shorter than others. In autumn, on the month of September the shadow will fall on the altar's entrance. This is the emperor's birthday, and yours. You will be exactly five when that shadow comes, so don't be scared,' she said comfortingly. The boy screamed remained fearful; 'The gods are watching me, they are. See that eye on the stone'. His mother chuckled, 'That is Egyptian writing, and this was erected in honour of the sun god. That standing stone was brought all the way from Egypt by the emperor, and this shows how the emperor rules over that foreign land now'. She stroked her son's head, and he seemed content with her explanation.

Before Augustus' death in 13 CE, he was unable to keep up with the affairs in office, due to his ill health. The Senate created a committee, who would personally visit Augustus and discuss state affairs with him. The powers of the committee were equal to that of the whole Senate, and they voted on urgent matters when it was necessary to do so. One day, Augustus lay in his bed unable to move, and he instructed Tiberius to visit him. Augustus' hands shook, and he was unable to hold down meals. Livia nursed him, and when Tiberius entered his chamber, she left the men to discuss business. 'Tiberius,' said Augustus and paused. 'I have become very frail and unable to keep up with affairs of the state. I will need you as my successor to start taking responsibility for what is to come. I have ensured that you have the powers of the principate, so that the succession can occur smoothly,' he said as his voice wavered. 'Sir, I came to visit armies in Illyricum initially, and then went on to visit my father's tomb in Campania. A messenger came to me, and told me that your health was failing,' Tiberius commented with concern. Livia and Tiberius stayed by Augustus' side for days, watching him slowly slip away from the world. On the nineteenth of August, 14 CE, the emperor died, and the people in nearby Campania mourned the loss of their leader.

The locals of Campania accompanied the emperor's corpse as the procession made its way back to Rome. Before Augustus was to be cremated, all business ceased, and people from all around Italy and the provinces came to view the body. Newly elected Roman magistrates decided to take part in Augustus' funeral rites. Tiberius, and his son, Drusus, performed the eulogy and went to the cremation site Campus Martius, which was close to the mausoleum. Livia put the torch beneath Augustus, and the wax eagle that had accompanied the procession melted slowly as the flames rose, although superstitious people said that the eagle had come to life and flown up into the heavens, taking with it the dead emperor's spirit. A Senator called to Livia: 'I see the spirit of our leader being taken up by the gods'. Livia, pleased to hear this, awarded the man with one million sesterces. The Senate declared that Augustus had joined the gods, and had him deified. A new temple was erected in his honour, and along with it a new priesthood was created, called 'soldales Augustdales'. These priests would celebrate the cult of the defied leader, and it was hoped that this would help to bring security to the provinces that surrounded Italy. After five days, Livia obtained Augustus' ashes, taking them to their final resting place, and in the mausoleum, a life-sized statue of the emperor stood proud in armour, reminding Romans of his loyalty to the state.

After Augustus' death, the 'Res Gestae Divi Augusti' (the account of his achievements) was sent to all parts of Italy, and its surrounding provinces. The document, which was inscribed on stone tablets, and forged in bronze, outlined the emperor's accomplishments, and his praiseworthy actions performed on behalf of the empire. Although Augustus' autobiographical account was mostly written in his early years, he knew that death was awaiting him, so he made the final touches to it in 14 CE. Upon the emperor's death, the perpetual flame of Rome dimmed for a few hours. The Vestal Virgins were worried that this might be a bad omen for Rome, but as soon as Augustus' will and testament were presented to the Senate, the flame burnt bright once more. The bronze pillars, on which the 'Res Gestae Divi Augusti' were inscribed, were positioned at the front entrance of the mausoleum for all to see. As the years passed, the metal eroded, until it was most likely melted down during a siege of Rome. Despite the disappearance of the pillars, their imprints in the mausoleum can still be seen. In Galatia, the Roman general had the will and testament engraved into the minds of prominent families so that the words would not be forgotten. In other provinces the 'Res Gestae' was carved into stone tablets in both Latin and Greek, so that the locals were able to understand the significance of its message. In Ancrya especially, the document was produced in both languages on the outer walls in the Temple of Roma, which was dedicated to Augustus. This bilingual inscription was a symbol for the intertwining of Roman and Greek cultures. Three inscriptions remain, but none of them is completely intact, but by piecing the puzzle together, modern people are able to understand its significance.

A young Senator, by the name of Livius, studied the 'Res Gestae' before sending it to the territories, and concluded that the text raised Augustus up to a god like-status. Whilst examining the text, he spoke with his good friend and advisor, Atius. Livius called over Atius, and showed the learned man the 'Res Gestae'. 'It does not account for all the events that happened between Caesar's death, and Augustus succession. There is no mention of Antonius or other rivals with whom he dealt,' he said. Atius nodded in agreement, saying, 'The Res Gestae is an honourific text, which is designed to outline the political achievements and awards bestowed upon the emperor. If he speaks too much of his failures, he would not have been deified by the Senate. I know that you were one of the committee members who questioned his decisions, and voted accordingly, but you must let your personal experiences go. It is a matter of what is good for the principate, and for the people. He must be remembered as a hero, not as a butcher. As he promised, he brought peace to Rome, and for the first time in centuries the gates of Janus remained closed.' Livius explained: 'This is the legacy that Augustus has left us. Atius, he is the first dictator to rule for a period of forty years, and avoided being assassinated like his father. Although people did try to kill him, he was wise, and wore his armour to public events.' Venus was overjoyed at Augustus' success both in life, and in death. The gods favoured Rome, and ensured that peace would last for another two hundred years.

Atius, much older than Livius, was present when the 'Res Gestae' was composed in its two stages, in 2 BCE and in 13 CE. 'Livius, Augustus surely wanted to outshine his predecessors, which is why the text emphasises him in a favourable light. I have read all thirty-five chapters of the 'Res Gestae' but it can be divided into four major parts,' Atius said knowingly. Livius shook his head, and stated that the text was something greater than that. 'As Augustus wrote the account, he pictured Romans standing in awe of his achievements. This is why in chapters one to fourteen he dealt with the honours that were bestowed upon him.' Livius picked up the document and started to read the following:

Annos undeviginti natus exercitum private consilio et private impensa comparavi, per quem rem publicam a dominatione factionis oppressam in libertatem vindicavi... Eo [nomi]ne senates decretis honorif[i]cis in ordinem suum m[e aldegit C(aio) et Pansa et A(ulo) Hirrit]o consulibus con[sula]rem locum s[ententiae dicendae simu]l [dans et i]mperium mihi dedit... Res publica n[e quid detrimen-

ti caperet], me pro praetor simul cum consulibus pro[vi-
dere iussit... p]opulus autem eodem anno me consulem,
cum [consul uterqu]e in bel[lo ceci] disset, et triumvirum
rei publicae consituend[ae creavit]. (Cooley, 2009, p. 58).

In English this translates to:

> Aged nineteen years old [44 BCE] I mustered an army at my
> personal decision and at my personal expense, and with it I
> liberated the state, which had been oppressed by despotic
> faction...For this reason the senate passed [honourif-
> ic] decrees admitting me to its body in the consul-
> ship of [Caius] Pansa and Aulus Hirtius [43 BCE], at the
> same time giving me consular precedence in stating my
> opinion, and it gave me supreme command...To pre-
> vent the state from suffering harm, it ordered me as
> propraetor to take precautions together with the con-
> suls...In the same year [43 BCE], moreover, the people
> appointed me consul, after both consuls had fallen in
> war, and triumvir for settling state. (Cooley, 2009, p. 58).

Atius disagreed with Livius' view on the matter, and explained
that Augustus had also detailed the amount of money spent
at his personal expense for the benefit of Rome in chapters
fifteen to twenty-five. 'Livius, he wanted to be remembered
as a selfless leader who only thought about the benefit of
the Roman people, yet in chapters twenty-six to thirty-three
he outlined the 'Pax Romana', which outlined his military and
diplomatic achievements. We should be grateful for the peace
and security he has brought Rome,' Atius remarked. Livius
agreed, and read out the final part of the text, which was obviously designed to be a eulogy at his funeral. 'As father of the
people, he protected Rome like a daughter,' he commented.

Atius thought about Augustus' military accolades and diplomatic achievements, pondering why he had failed to mention

victory over his rivals, Lepidus, Antonius and Pompeius. Livius questioned what was on Atius' mind. 'I was thinking about how Augustus failed to mention his rivals, which we know was done for a purpose, but surely Rome would be proud of his victory over Antonius, who was seduced by that foreign queen. Ah, yes, the slave revolt that he mentions here in this text is in reference to Pompeius. He obviously would not mention the massacre of Varrus' legions, the proscriptions, and his failure to conquer Sabaeans of Arabia,' stated Atius.

'This is true enough, Atius, but he also failed to approach the subject of his 'Maius Imperium Proconsulare', where he held supreme control over other proconsuls. Augustus reiterates time and time again about how he benefited the republic, which we both know was a ploy to keep him alive. You see, Atius, to admit that he was a dictator would have made him a target for assassination. Interestingly, Augustus was not afraid to speak of the use of 'Tribunician Potestas', which gave him the power to have legislations enacted on his behalf,' Livius remarked. 'That is only because the tribunate was a voice for the people,' Atius added. 'I can't help but wonder what Venus would think of his actions. Was he just or corrupt? I think that the former best embodies our emperor's character.' Livius nodded in agreement.

To win five civil wars, Augustus had gained the reputation among his enemies, and those who were intelligent enough to perceive his true colours, saw him as being a severe, cruel and treacherous individual. As far as Augustus was concerned, his reputation could not stay that way, so he had appealed to the poets and writers of Rome to write about him in a favourable light. According to Augustus' enemies, a praetor, Quintus Gallius, was suspected of approaching the princeps with a sword concealed beneath his robe. Rumour had it that Augustus first tortured the man in the same way as a slave, and tore out his eyes with his own hands, before having the man executed. Such defamation had to be dealt with promptly, and Augustus formed his own version of the tale. According to the emperor, Gallius was suspected of conspiring against him, but he was given a fair trial and sentenced to banishment, and by some mishap died on his way to exile. Other rumours also needed to be refuted. People had whispered in the streets as Augustus passed them, and Agrippa informed him that people were gossiping about his cowardly behaviour in the civil wars, whereby he was said to have abandoned his men at Philippi. It was true enough that sickness prevented Augustus from taking an active part in the war, but people questioned why he was not found in his litter. The story told by Augustus was that one of his friends had experienced a vision in which he should rise from his bed and depart from the camp. Those who were superstitious may have believed in the divine vision, but most questioned his actions. In his autobiography, Augustus acknowledged that he had almost been overthrown by an insurrection amongst his men, which distracted him causing him to put his boot on the wrong foot. Mistakes like these were excusable, but he had to answer for less than desirable actions at Actium, which he struggled to explain in his account.

Whilst the emperor had difficulty excusing his actions at Actium, he was more than happy to exaggerate his achievements against the tribes of Illyria. His account says he brought back insurgents and had them applaud him. Augustus boasted of his victory over the crude, war-like people of the Alps who had often pillaged and plundered Italy. Despite his over-inflated opinion of himself, there is a degree of apologetic tone in his autobiography. The opponents of Augustus took every opportunity to paint him in a negative light, especially where his victories were concerned, yet he portrays himself as the virtuous saviour of Rome. He was depicted by some as cruel, savage and selfish, but he empahasised his forgivable nature, for it was Augustus who took the children of his enemies and raised them with his sister Octavia. Others attacked his legal procedures, yet he was the one who passed social laws for the benefit of Roman families. Many condemned him for his actions against Antonius, who was once a friend, and for the exile of his own daughter, though Augustus stressed his loyalty towards those close to him. There were exceptions to the rule; Augustus had been unable to live peacefully with Scribonia, and he hoped that the Roman populace would understand that she was a disagreeable individual.

Augustus may have overlooked the individual's plight in his autobiography. Just imagine Quintius Gallius' life story and why he may have wanted to kill Augustus. Gallius was born to parents Q. Gallius and Herita, in 64 BCE and was twenty years old when Iulius Caesar died. Though a similar age to Augustus, his viewpoint differed greatly from that of the patricians and the Senate. Gallius may have been born to a struggling plebeian family, and his mother would tell him the tales of his grandfather who went to war for Sulla, and was then proscribed and put to death by the same man he fought for. Gallius would see friends proscribed by Augustus in the hopes of getting financial remuneration. The proscriptions affected him personally, as he lost his betrothed in the bloodbath instigated by Antonius, Augustus (then Octavianus), and Lepidus. His hatred of authority was fuelled by the loss of his father in Gaul, and despite his father being in the army for almost twenty years, he lost his life before he was granted his land allotment. Gallius was angry about this, and felt that his father had died in vain.

Tears welled in his eyes, as he thought about the unfortunate situation that affected his family. Gallia, his sister, had been forced by Augustan social reforms to marry two years after her husband died at Actium. Gallia, having been deeply in love with her first husband, resented her second marriage, and Gallius understood the grief she was experiencing. Though the average Roman lived in the expectance of death, it still did not make the grieving process any easier. Gallius, friend to his brother-in-law, started to loathe Augustus for what he had done. Coming from a family who worshipped the republican ideal, he saw that Augustus was nothing more than a cruel autocrat. As time passed, he wished to do something about this young would-be emperor.

Whilst talking with his sister, he found that she was very unhappy in her marriage. 'Gallia, I'm sorry that you have had to marry again', Gallius commented. She stated that a lot had changed and that this was the life she had to be content with now. 'Antonius was one of Iulius Caesar's best generals, yet Octavianus betrayed him by declaring war on Egypt, and as a result you have lost the love of your life'. 'Gallius, Caius had pledged his allegiance to Antonius, and did not betray his general's trust, like so many others', she said tearfully and paused. 'Because Caius was at war, I bore him no children, and was subject to the new reforms; if I had had my way I wouldn't have married for another couple of years.' She explained that she didn't want to marry for the sake of it. Gallia was hoping to find a nice equite, who would provide for her and her family. Instead, she was forced to marry the son of a fisherman. Her brother's anger grew, and he could not contain his feelings about the matter. Everything they had tried to do to advance their family had failed. Both Gallius and Gallia were prisoners to their class and their fate had been sealed.

Army recruitment was lessening as there were no longer any civil wars to fight, so Gallius was subject to the corn dole. The corn dole was a socialist reform brought in by late republicans so that unemployed people would not go hungry. With no job prospects, and having failed to follow in his father's military footsteps, life seemed bleak. At least his sister had been able to marry a man who had a trade and, even though they were poor, rent was paid every week. Gallius had only the corn dole to keep the wolf from the door, and he had no fixed address. Augustus grew rich, as he stayed poor, to Gallius' resentment. Augustus had everything a man could want: wealth, fame, noble bloodlines, and the power to change the world. Gallius had no wife, as he could not provide for one, let alone any children they might have. His sister sympathised with Scribonia, as she had been poorly treated by Augustus. Nothing was done to address the mass unemployment, and this made Gallius desperate. As a man who could not afford to buy shoes for his feet, he had to steal in order to get by. He was in and out of prison, paying for being poor.

Gallius had a good reason for wanting to assassinate Augustus, and dressed himself like a soldier so that he could get close enough to make an attempt on the emperor's life. One of Augustus' colleagues saw the glint of bronze in the sunlight and pulled him back from his attacker. Gallius was wrestled to the ground and his hands were tied with cord. Gallia requested to see her brother in prison, but was denied this right. Augustus did not want him conspiring with anyone else in the aftermath of an assassination attempt. Sure enough, his fingers were cut off one by one, and he was questioned as to his intentions. 'Who hired you?' Agrippa questioned. Gallius informed that he had intended to kill Augustus for his own reasons. Not believing his confession, the torture continued. Word travelled through the plebeians that a Roman citizen was being tortured like a slave and discontented crowds began to gossip. Augustus ruthlessly gouged out the eyes of Gallius and ordered his execution. His body was so badly mutilated that it was unrecognisable, so in an attempt to hide the murder they dumped Gallius' remains in an aqueduct. Whilst this may not be Gallius story, there are no other sources accept for Augustus' account to be relied on and it is clear that he exaggerated things in his own favour.

After the death of the aged emperor, rumours lessened, and the 'Res Gestae Divi Augusti' became accepted as fact in Rome and her provinces. As generations passed, Augustus was remembered for his triumphs and reign of peace. Tales of people like Quintus Gallius became only rumours and there were no discernible facts on which to base an accurate story. Who knows what happened to the average plebeian? Slowly, with time and erosion, some of the 'Res Gestae Divi Augusti' was lost. Fourteen years prior to Augustus' death, a new saviour was born, or so the story is told. Certainly, Augustus lived through the birth of Jesus Christ and Tiberius' reign probably condemned the king of the Jews to death. Augustus was careful not to call himself an emperor or king as there had been hundreds of years of hatred of monarchs, which was the reason for Iulius Caesar's assassination.

As time went on, stories of these legendary figures would come have remained influential to modern society two thousand years later. We owe our democratic ideals to Rome, and the shape of her Republic still echoes in western politics. The greatest question is whether Rome ever fell, or did it merely transform into the Byzantine Empire, and then into the Catholic Church? Rome was not only the founder of modern politics, but was also responsible for the beginning of Christianity. If it had not been for great historical figures like Augustus, the world today would be quite different. Augustus was a turning point in the ancient world, and two thousand years have born witness to so many marvels and atrocities. Augustus, above all else, brought about peace for Rome, and the Italian provinces. Many forget about the rocky foundations on which this peace was forged.